A DICKENS OF A CHRISTMAS NOVEL
BY LAURA ROLLINS

ALSO BY LAURA ROLLINS

Lockhart Regency Romance

Courting Miss Penelope—available at LauraRollins.com

Wager for a Lady's Hand

Lily for my Enemy

A Heart in the Balance

A Farewell Kiss

A Well-Kept Promise

A Dickens of a Christmas

The Hope of Christmas Past

The Joy of Christmas Present

The Peace of Christmas Yet to Come

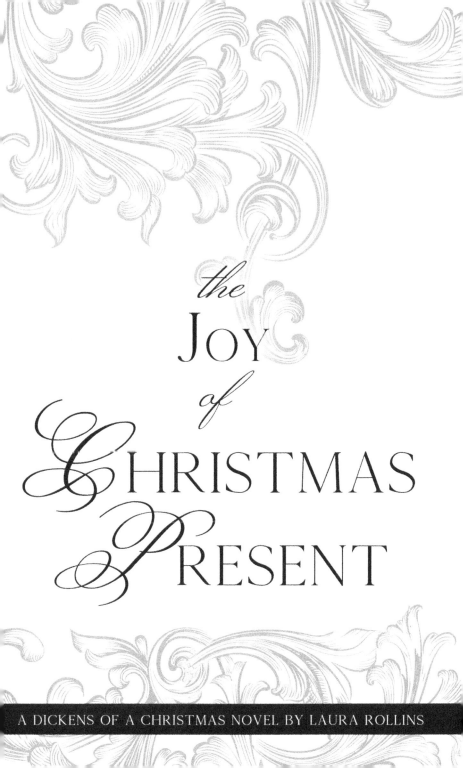

Copyright © 2020 by Laura Rollins

All rights reserved.

No part of this book may be reproduced in any form or by any electronic or mechanical means, including information storage and retrieval systems, without written permission from the author, except for the use of brief quotations in a book review.

NOTE FROM THE AUTHOR

Some time ago, the thought came to me to create a trilogy based on Charles Dickens's *A Christmas Carol*. However, in making one book become three stories, a single fact became immediately clear. This would not be a retelling in the truest sense of the word.

This is not a book about a grumpy old man who is visited by spirits in the middle of the night and awakes the next day a better individual.

Instead, I decided to take the essence of the three spirits and write one story around each of them. I wanted to take the messages told by the Ghost of Christmas Past, the Ghost of Christmas Present, and the Ghost of Christmas Yet to Come and explore the lessons and ideas they present.

That being said, many of the characters first imagined by Charles Dickens make cameo appearances here and there, though I have taken some liberties to aid in telling these stories.

I believe it is worth mentioning that some of the holiday terms we now use to reference the Christmas season were either not used in Regency times, used in slightly different ways, or used to mean slightly different things. Unfortunately, many resources were contradictory on this point—in those cases, I deferred to Dickens's *A Christmas Carol* and the complete works of Jane Austen.

After much research, here is a list of terms and how they are used in this series:

"Christmas"—refers to the entire season, not simply one day.

"Christmas time"—Dickens uses this term, but always as two words (not the "Christmastime" we are used to seeing).

"Holyday"—a formal term used to reference specific religious days, including, but not limited to Epiphany, Ash Wednesday, Good Friday, Easter, Whitsunday, and Christmas Day.

"Merry Christmas"—used by Dickens. The term "Happy Christmas" only became popular later.

"Christmas holidays" and "jolly holidays"—though often in England the term "holiday" refers to a break from school and work during the summer, both Dickens and Austen use the term "Christmas holidays" and Dickens even once says "jolly holidays," so I chose to include both terms in this story as well.

"Greetings of the season," "festive season," "the season," and "winter season"—all also show up in Dickens's and Austen's stories.

I hope you find this story memorable and that it brings a bit more light to your jolly holidays!

Merry Christmas and God bless us every one.

To Kelli,
Who chooses Joy,
regardless of what the days bring.

"Come in!" exclaimed the Ghost. "Come in! and know me better, man!"

Scrooge entered timidly, and hung his head before this Spirit. He was not the dogged Scrooge he had been; and though the Spirit's eyes were clear and kind, he did not like to meet them.

"I am the Ghost of Christmas Present," said the Spirit. "Look upon me!"

A Christmas Carol
by Charles Dickens

CHAPTER ONE

Late April, 1813

Lord Fredrick Chapman opened the study door but didn't enter. The whole room—the musky smell that lingered, the heavy desk along one wall, the forest green rug and walnut furniture—it all reminded him far too much of Father.

Father, who'd died not five weeks ago.

Fredrick placed a hand on the door frame and rested his head against it. Blast, but tears still felt embarrassingly close to the surface. At least, for the moment, he was alone—a circumstance that came but rarely now. Sighing loudly, he pushed off the door frame and strode into the study.

He got no further than the middle of the rug. Father used to sit in here for hours each day, seeing to matters of Parliament, engaging in heated debates with the other lords he invited over, or simply hiding from Fredrick's twin sisters, Christina and Eleanor, when they were most bent on discussing lace, fashion, and eligible bachelors. Fredrick ran a hand down the back of his neck, pulling on the tension there. He'd hidden in here *with* Father any number of times.

Fredrick's hand dropped back to his side. The room was his now. The whole house, in the best part of London, no less, was his. So was the country estate, the hunting lodge up North, and several smaller estates scattered across England. It felt like it all —houses, land, everything—had settled onto his shoulders, crushing him into the ground. He reached out and placed a hand against the wingback closest to him. How was he ever to manage?

See to the various estates and tenant problems? Lead in Parliament as his father had done? And, above all else, care for a grieving mother and two sisters who were supposed to be enjoying their first ever London Season? Instead, they were wearing black and turning down invitations to balls and musicales. It wasn't right; yet, he couldn't fix it.

He couldn't fix any of it.

Steps sounded just outside the door. A footman ducked in.

"Mr. Baker and Miss Baker to see you, sir."

His uncle and cousin had come? Again? Fredrick pulled himself up straight. "Show them in." Father had always made sure his younger brother—Mr. Baker—and his family wanted for nothing. That, too, would be his responsibility now.

"Fredrick," Baker said, walking quickly over to him, "Good to see you. Good to see you."

"Same to you, sir." Fredrick clasped the older man's hand in his own and gave it a solid shake.

Miss Alice Baker trailed directly behind her father. "How are my aunt and dear cousins today?" She spoke on before Fredrick could answer. "I must speak with them—I have such the greatest *on-dit* to share." Her eyes sparked in the way they only did when Alice was sharing gossip, which happened more often than not.

"Hold on there," Baker said to his daughter. "I had rather

thought you'd want to be present when I give Fredrick the good news."

News? Fredrick's stomach grew hard. He was sick to death of "news." News was how it had all started.

His father was feeling ill. His mother insisted the situation was not so grave as all that. The doctor had been called.

There was nothing anyone could do.

Alice's eyes grew wide. "You mean you have not discussed this with him?" Her gaze moved to Fredrick and she laughed. "I had rather thought it a done deal."

"What is a done deal?" Fredrick asked, confident he truly didn't want to know.

"My boy." Baker clapped Fredrick on the shoulder. "Your father, may he rest in peace, always looked out for me and mine. He was a true brother and a true friend."

Fredrick felt the familiar sting of tears against the back of his eyes. Why was it that society only believed tears belonged to the fairer sex? When a beloved father passed, shouldn't *all* be allowed to grieve? But, no. If a gentleman cried, it meant he was weak and incapable—two things Fredrick could not afford to be.

Baker continued. "So, in honor of your dear father, I have decided to help you in kind."

"That is not—"

Baker held up a hand. "It is the least I can do, believe me."

All right then. Fredrick probably should have been pleased to know Uncle was willing to help him out in some way; he was feeling quite drowned by all his responsibilities at the moment.

Fredrick found he couldn't feel easy with Alice grinning like a hungry cat, but he had been raised to be polite. "Thank you," he said. "In what way are you insisting you help me?"

He sounded a bit ungrateful. He wasn't—he was just overwhelmed and not at all in the mood for games.

Baker's smile grew. "Fred, my boy"—two 'my boys' in one

conversation could not purport anything good—"I have found you a wife."

"A what?" Fredrick all but shouted. Taking a half step back, his elbow bumped against the wingback chair.

Alice giggled. "Isn't it perfect! She's not whom I would have considered the right woman for you—after all, she is a bit on the shelf—but I am sure once you see her, you will think nothing at all the matter since she *is* rather pretty in her own right, and though she doesn't care for the pianoforte, I hear she is quite adept at the harp, though I don't think society will ever truly accept a woman who wants to play the harp instead of the pianoforte—"

"Oh, hush, Alice," Baker said.

Fredrick simply stared. A wife? Was his uncle mad? Perhaps deranged from grief? Fredrick had felt himself slipping toward Bedlam more than once these past weeks. There was always a chance Uncle had beat him there.

"She is a fine lady," Baker said, either ignorant or uncaring that Fredrick could hardly make sense of the words falling from his mouth. "Comes from an upstanding family, a long line of titles and the like." He gave Alice a small nudge with his shoulder.

"Oh, yes," she jumped in eagerly. "Miss Helena Spencer is a beautiful woman. Very . . . good on the harp. And blonde. She has blonde hair. And she smiles. A lot. So you should like that. And she also lost her father not too long ago, so you have something in common. Or was it her mother who just died?"

"Her mother died in childbirth." Baker corrected in a hushed voice. "Her father passed last year."

"Oh, that's right. Silly me," Alice said with what felt to Fredrick like a stark lack of concern for Miss Spencer's plight.

He could not even begin to delineate all the things he saw wrong with Alice's "compliments" toward this lady who was supposedly perfect for him.

"Baker," Fredrick started, "thank you"—was it a sin to thank a person when one had never been less thankful?—"but I cannot, in good conscience, agree to marry any lady whom I have never before laid eyes on."

"Well, if you need to see her is all," Baker shrugged, "that can easily be arranged."

Seeing the lady was not the issue. Not by far.

But, if Uncle didn't get that on his own, then Fredrick did not have the energy to elaborate until he did.

"I am still in mourning," Fredrick tried. "I cannot court or wed. Not for eleven months still."

"Oh, poo." Baker chuckled. "Many a man weds before the full year is up. The important thing is that Miss Spencer will be out of mourning in a couple of months, and then you two can wed before removing to the country this autumn."

He was serious. The deuced man was actually serious.

"No," Fredrick said. Hang his tutor's lessons on politeness. This needed to end now. "I am not interested."

"But you need a wife, and so I have found you one." Baker looked genuinely confused at Fredrick's refusal.

"Last year," Alice started, her creased brow a comical replica of her father's, "you said my friend Elizabeth was blessed to have such things arranged for her. Father and I were led to believe you might think such a thing a blessing for you as well."

"This is nothing like Mr. and Mrs. Weston's match." In that situation, both parties had kept company many times and were quite agreeable to the arrangement—they hadn't had it foisted upon them without warning. Besides, he'd only said as much to Alice because he knew Mr. Weston to be the best sort of man, in hopes that it would calm his cousin's dramatics.

Baker sighed. "Her guardian will be most disappointed."

Her guardian? "You haven't spoken with the man, have you?"

"Of course I have. With her father gone, Lord Shakerley has taken her in. He is the nearest thing she has to a male relation and the one seeing to her well-being. Who else would I have spoken to? Her?"

Fredrick groaned. "No, Uncle, but you could have spoken to *me*. You had no right to speak on *my* behalf."

Baker's tone turned petulant. "I was only trying to help my brother's son. My own nephew."

"I know," Fredrick said. As much as he could not like what Uncle had done, he knew he had acted out of love. Gads, what would father have done in such a situation?

"You have quite a load on your shoulders," Baker said softly. "Of that I have no doubt."

"Father was the best man I have ever known," Fredrick said, clasping his hands behind his back. "I'm not sure I'll ever carry it as well as he did." His gaze dropped momentarily to the rug beneath their feet. Could someone like himself ever measure up? Was such a feat even possible?

"Do my aunt and cousins have plans for this hunting season?" Alice asked. "If you are wanting to remove yourself to the hunting lodge, they can come stay with us."

The corner of Fredrick's mouth turned up in a half-smile. "They will be pleased to know you have thought of them. But no, my plans are to have the whole family removed to the country estate. I will stay with Mother until she no longer needs me."

Alice smiled. "You're a good son."

No, he was simply the only son his mother had. The only brother his sisters could claim. The only one who could step in where his father had left off. He only prayed he didn't disappoint them too greatly.

Baker pulled out a thick, folded bit of paper. "Lord Shakerley will be sad to know I cannot return this with your signature."

"Excuse me?" Fredrick's pulse quickened, beating hard against his throat. "You'd gotten so far as to write up a contract?" Lud, this was far worse than he thought.

"Well, yes, we both thought the two of you would make an excellent match. What else were we to do?"

"Not this." A contract, even one not signed, implied there was a connection between them. It meant people *expected* a wedding. It meant rumors and gossip.

Fredrick's gaze jumped between Baker and Alice. "Who all knows of this?" He could only pray there weren't many.

"Lord Shakerley, us . . ." Baker's voice trailed off.

Alice didn't say anything at all.

"Does *she* know? Miss Spencer, I mean?"

Baker's brow creased. "I am not certain. His lordship didn't give me the details on what she has been informed of and what she hasn't."

Fredrick certainly hoped she hadn't been apprised of any of it. Either way, it wasn't as though Miss Spencer had her heart riding on Fredrick. How could she? They'd never met.

"You need to speak with Lord Shakerley immediately. Let him know that this is not going to happen."

"Are you sure?" Baker pressed. "Securing a wife for one's self can be time consuming. Why not let me do this bit for you? As earl now, it is your responsibility to produce an heir."

Fredrick clamped his mouth shut to keep from saying something he'd regret later. "I am sure, Uncle. I thank you for your consideration, but I ask that you allow me to handle my own romances from here on out."

"If that's what you wish."

"Yes, that is exactly what I wish." Fredrick was losing the battle to remain calm and collected. He could feel it. "And I think it best if you go right away."

"Well, perhaps the man could see me tomorrow. If not, surely the next—"

"*Now*, Uncle. This very minute."

Baker slipped the contract back inside his jacket. "Very well. Come, Alice." The two moved quickly toward the door, daughter trailing, wordless, after her father.

Fredrick's cousin was acting rather silent—a very strange occurrence for her. He found it unsettling.

"Alice," Fredrick called, "*no one* knows about this, correct?"

She pursed her lips tightly together and nodded, only a small "Mm-hmm" coming from her. Then the two were gone, their footsteps echoing down the corridor as they left.

Fredrick circled the wingback and sat heavily in it. Of all the nodcock notions. He hid his eyes behind a hand. Uncle choosing him a wife? How could a grown man—one with a wife and family of his own—not see how undesirable such an act would be?

Removing his mother and sisters to the country was clearly the best move. They'd be away from matchmaking matrons, meddling family, and all of it. In the country, Fredrick felt certain they would all find the peace they needed to grieve properly. There was nothing else for it; he would see them all out of London and on their way before sunset tomorrow.

He could only hope that Alice had spoken truthfully. When it came to Uncle and his crazed idea, Fredrick sincerely hoped that no one would ever know the match had even been considered.

CHAPTER TWO

Seven months later

*E*veryone knew.
  Miss Helena Spencer could feel it. In the way the servants had glanced at her as they'd hurried to bring her trunks upstairs. In the way her hostess's eyes had widened when Lady Emma Shakerley, a lifelong friend, had introduced her. In the way all the other house guests had stilled at the sound of her name and stopped to stare.

Everyone knew.

They knew she'd been engaged, or nearly. They knew the gentleman—one Lord Chapman—had fled to the country rather than marry her. They had read all the papers, seen the mortifying caricatures depicting her being cast aside. Sometimes the gossip columns had hinted that she was too ugly, other times that she was a horrid singer; still others and insinuated far more vulgar falsehoods.

If either of her parents were still alive, they would have been appalled at the happenings of last Season. Helena herself could hardly face her own reflection in the mirror. She'd gone to Town as Emma's guest, both as a means of meeting people and to distract herself from her loss, but also to ensure she ate more than a bit of bread a day as all her father's estate had been entailed away. London had been full of joyful diversions and had gone a long way to help Helena feel more like herself.

Then everything had come crashing down around her.

She'd never felt so alone.

The hollowed-out feeling the scandal brought hadn't left since, even months later.

"Perhaps," Emma addressed their hostess, Lady Andrews, even while looping an arm through Helena's, "you might have a maid show us to our rooms? We've had quite the trip and want to rest before dinner."

"Oh, yes." Lady Andrews seemed to shake off the stupor that hearing Helena's name had caused. "Certainly, you will want to freshen up." Their hostess was a tall woman, a bit of gray along her temples, and appeared congenial. Would her good nature stretch so far as to see past the rumors and gossip that followed Helena everywhere she went? She could only hope . . . and wait . . . to find out.

A maid was summoned and not five minutes later, Helena was sitting in the room prepared for Emma—her own room only next door—and relaxing against the settee.

"I can't believe I let you talk me into this." Helena sighed, tipping her head back and closing her eyes. She'd known venturing out into society, even for a simple Christmas house party, was not without risks. But since she'd been living with the Shakerleys since her father's passing over a year ago, she couldn't have refused to come, not when Emma and both her parents had been so insistent that she do so.

"It wasn't that bad," Emma hedged.

Helena's head came back up, and she skewered Emma with her most pointed scowl.

"All right." Emma sighed. "But at least now you have the

worst behind you. Mother assured me that Lady Andrews always keeps her house parties small and only invites the most honorable of individuals to Hedgewood Manor. To be numbered among the group will certainly be a boon to your reputation."

"My *shattered* reputation, you mean."

"Oh, come now," Emma huffed.

Helena turned in the chair and faced Emma directly. "If I didn't know any better, I'd say, judging by the expression on Lady Andrews's face when you introduced us, that she had no idea you were bringing me along."

Emma waggled her shoulders up and down. "I wrote to her and said I was bringing a dear friend."

"*A dear friend?* All the while conveniently forgetting to mention that *I* was that friend?"

"Once the other guests have gotten a chance to know you, they will quickly see that the papers and the rumors got you all wrong. You'll see."

Helena shook her head. "I hope you're right. Otherwise this will be a most miserable month."

"Good!" Emma rushed suddenly to Helena's side. "Then you're not crying off?"

"Excuse me?"

"I was certain the moment you found out what I'd done—or rather, what I'd not done—that you'd be packed and gone again."

"Then why did you not tell Lady Andrews?" Helena held up a hand. "Wait, don't answer that." Helena knew full well why Emma hadn't felt like she could tell their hostess who her dear friend was.

Emma took hold of Helena's hand and squeezed it. "I'm so glad you're staying." Then she stood and hurried over to her bed and flung herself down on it. "We're going to have the most diverting Christmastide ever; I can feel it."

Emma was forever *feeling* things; the woman's premonitions were never-ending, if not completely infallible.

No matter what Lady Andrews's thoughts upon seeing a scandal-laden lady at her own house party, Emma wasn't the only person who hadn't been fully open and honest.

Though she hadn't breathed a word of it to anyone, Helena had agreed to come for reasons far more important than claiming inclusion at one of Lady Andrews's enviable house parties.

"You know," Emma said with a yawn, "that was truly an exhausting trip."

Helena stood. "How about you get that rest you told Lady Andrews we needed?"

"Where are you going?" Emma asked, lifting no more than her head off the pillows below her.

"Just to my own room. Don't worry; I have little desire to wander about the estate alone." Helena was far less confident that the other guests would grow to accept her than Emma was.

"Very well. We can go down to dinner together."

"Sounds lovely." Helena slipped from the room and opened the door to her own bedchamber. Jane, her abigail, was hurrying about, unpacking and putting everything into place. The young woman was a marvel. Helena didn't know how she managed to make Helena feel like she'd brought a little bit of home no matter where they traveled. Since Helena was at the disposal of Lady Emma Shakerley, they traveled quite a bit.

"Almost finished, miss," Jane said with a curtsy. "Do you wish me to finish now or leave you with some peace?"

Was it horribly selfish insisting her abigail stop what she was doing when it would only require she come back later to finish? But Helena desperately needed some solitude at the moment. Hopefully, she wouldn't be putting Jane out too much.

"I think I would like a nap," Helena said.

Jane curtsied once more and then slipped from the room. The stillness which enveloped Helena was both welcomed and sad. After all that had happened to her nearly seven months ago, Helena had never wanted for family so badly.

She'd never known her mother since she'd died giving birth to Helena. But she and Father had made a family of just the two of them. They'd rarely been apart for any length of time. Then he'd grown ill. Doctor after doctor had been called, but none had been able to help. He'd passed away in his sleep, leaving Helena quite alone in the world.

Yes, she had Emma and Lord and Lady Shakerley. But they weren't family. They weren't bound to care for her. Though she sincerely appreciated all they'd done, Helena couldn't shake the feeling that she didn't fully belong with them. They would always be dear friends, but they'd *only* ever be friends.

Helena moved to her unpacked trunk and pushed a few items of clothing aside. Near the bottom was the letter she'd written three weeks ago when Emma had first told her they would be staying with Lord and Lady Andrews over the holidays.

She'd never sent it though, for fear that Lady Andrews would turn her away the moment she arrived.

Lady Andrews had certainly been surprised at learning Helena had come, but she hadn't seemed on the verge of sending her away. That might still change, but for now, Helena was staying closer to the small town of Dunwell than she ever had before. There was a very good chance she would never be this close again. If ever she was going to act, now was the time.

Helena turned the letter over but didn't open it. She knew the contents too well. She'd written and rewritten the missive countless times. She'd simply been too scared that she might say the wrong thing.

How did one go about introducing oneself to an estranged

uncle? Helena's father had been an only child, but her mother had been one of two. She'd had a brother—one Helena had never met and who her father had only mentioned twice in all her life. When he'd passed, Helena had found the uncle's name and address among her father's possessions.

This uncle was her only living relative. Her only family.

Did he ever think of her? Know that her father had passed and that she was without family besides him? After the funeral, Helena had rather expected some kind of a message from him. Surely he realized that she was alone in the world now.

Did he even know she existed?

Helena had no idea. She walked slowly toward a small, well-placed desk beneath a tall window. The view looked out over a pond with a fountain in the middle, a lovely rose garden to the side of that, and beyond them both, a tall and stately hedge maze. The Andrews were certainly not ones to hire incompetent gardeners. If nothing else, perhaps one of these days Helena would simply wander into the hedge maze and get lost forever. She could slip from existence in a blaze of gossip.

Shaking the nonsense from her head, Helena sat and pulled out a quill pen. Blessedly, Jane had already unpacked her writing things and put the desk to rights.

Glancing at the slip of paper she'd found among her father's things, she turned the letter over and addressed it. She wouldn't send it today. She wanted to make it through at least one dinner before assuring her uncle that she could meet with him at his earliest convenience. She could only hope it would be quite soon. Helena needed family—even estranged family—now, more than ever before.

Careful to keep her pen steady, Helena added the gentleman's name above the address:

Mr. Ebenezer Scrooge.

CHAPTER THREE

*E*mma knocked on Helena's door just in time for dinner, as she'd promised. She truly was blessed to have such a dear friend in Emma.

"I am ready," Helena said.

But Emma wouldn't let her step out into the corridor; instead, she studied Helena's hair and gown from her position in the doorway.

"Is that what you've chosen to wear tonight?"

Helena glanced down at her simple, cream-colored dress. The answer was rather obvious. "Is it not to your liking?"

Emma placed a hand on her shoulder and pushed her back into her bedchamber.

Helena laughed lightly. "I had not thought Jane did such a bad job as all that."

Emma pursed her lips, still eying Helena closely. "No, you look lovely." The words came out as though Emma wasn't sure of her own pronouncement.

"Then what is the problem?"

"Do you . . . perhaps . . . feel you look, um, *too* lovely?"

What was that supposed to mean?

Emma lifted both hands up. "Please don't misunderstand. I know you to be of the highest moral standards."

Moral standards? Helena had been the subject of many such talks among her nosy neighbors, but she'd never expected it from her best friend.

"Only understand," Emma continued, "no one here knows you like I do."

"Your parents are here."

"Besides them." Emma pushed Helena in front of a full-length mirror. "What do you see?"

Helena wasn't at all sure what her friend expected her to say. She looked herself over for a minute and then shrugged. "A woman in a nice dress with curly auburn hair."

"Yes, but imagine you had been told that the woman there," Emma pointed to Helena's reflection in the mirror, "was not the kind one should allow into polite society. Imagine that woman there had made her way into your house party without your knowledge, and you had no idea if she was going to soil your own good name or not."

"Emma, you're being ridiculous."

"Oh, fine. I'll say it this way. I love your dress and I love your hair. But if I'd heard unseemly things about you—and of course only if I didn't already know you—I might wonder if your neckline wasn't a bit too low, and if you hadn't left more than an appropriate amount of your hair down around your shoulders."

"Emma," Helena growled. "*Your* neckline is lower than mine. And I've seen plenty of other women wear their hair half-down at dinner."

"That may be true, but don't you see how what may look innocent on another woman may give rise on you?"

Helena folded her arms. "This is all so very unfair." She'd been quite pleased with how she'd turned out this evening. Jane had taken extra care with her updo and Helena loved it. Her dress may not have been the most elegant thing she'd ever owned, but it was pretty and, more than that, she *felt* pretty when wearing it.

"Let us tuck a fichu into your neckline and I'll help you pin up a few of those lovely locks of yours and then you'll be perfectly presentable."

"I was presentable before you walked in," Helena huffed, but she sat at the dressing table anyway. As much as it galled her, Emma did have a point. Still, Helena didn't look in the mirror as she felt her friend pull and tug at her hair.

If only her father was still alive—he would have been able to stand up for her when Lord Chapman had walked out. More than that, he never would have considered the arrangement in the first place. He never would have agreed to meet with Lord Chapman's uncle, no papers would have been drawn up, and no possible connection would have made its way to the gossip mill.

Lord Shakerley had meant well, of course. And Helena bore him no ill will, though she couldn't quite say the same for the dubious Lord Chapman.

"There," Emma said after several minutes. "You still look quite beautiful."

Helena loved Emma, but she didn't trust her friend well enough to go down to dinner without looking at herself in the mirror first, no matter how much she wished she didn't have to.

It was as she feared. The dress was the same, but with the fichu—sheer and beautiful though it was—wrapped about her collarbone and tucked into her neckline, she looked far more like an aging matron than a young woman. Her hair was the same color, but Emma had pulled back pieces harshly and the up-do was no longer flattering.

"I certainly look staid," Helena said with a sigh.

"Which is exactly what we want," Emma said with a firm shake of her head. Catching sight of Helena's eyes, she reached out and took her hand. "It is only for tonight, and possibly tomorrow."

"And possibly the next day?"

"Only until we can show everyone here that you are all that is lovely and modest."

Helena ran a hand over the lace which came up fully to her throat. "If modest is what you were going for, I think you achieved it."

Emma clapped her hands. "Excellent. Let us go down now."

Helena followed her out and down the stairs but couldn't seem to muster the same enthusiasm as her friend. Emma had assured her that the stares and silence that had met Helena that afternoon, when they'd first arrived, would be the worst of it. But Helena wasn't convinced.

They entered the drawing room and found it comfortably full. It was not overly crowded, but there were plenty of people milling about.

Hadn't Emma said that Lady Andrews was known for hosting intimate house parties? This seemed a few too many individuals for such a thing, at least in Helena's mind.

Emma, bless her, did not leave Helena's side. Instead, she took Helena's hand and dragged her over to three handsome gentlemen to strike up a conversation. Apparently, Emma had met two of them in London earlier that year and had heard of the third. She wasted no time in introducing Helena.

There was Lord Ellis, tall and lean. He wore a black superfine over a dark green waistcoat. Simply put, he was a paragon. Helena could not remember ever meeting a man so beautiful. Nonetheless, while his smile was all things polite, his nose remained a bit lofty.

Next to him was Lord Dowding, a man of light brown hair and brilliant blue eyes who insisted both ladies simply call him Topper.

Lastly, was Lord Forbes. Shortest of the three men, his expression remained flat for the duration of their conversation and, though he carried a walking stick, Helena never once saw him put any weight on it.

If these three gentlemen had been in London for the Season, Helena knew they must realize who she was and what had happened. Whether they knew and chose to politely ignore all they'd heard, or they simply didn't care that they were keeping company with someone as tainted as she, Helena wasn't sure. Either way, they asked about her and Emma's trip; they showed interest in Emma's story over their carriage being stopped for nearly a quarter of an hour by a stray cow which refused to move out of their way; they even asked after Helena and her family, going so far as to express sympathy when they learned that both of her parents had passed.

All in all, Helena found herself relaxing. Perhaps Emma was right. Perhaps she'd allowed the scandal of before to box her in, to shut her away. Perhaps she should have reentered society before now. If these three gentlemen were any indication of what she should expect, then there was nothing truly to be afraid of.

Then, quite suddenly, the room grew still.

Helena glanced at Emma, but she only gave her a small shrug, a clear expression that she had no idea what was happening either.

Together, they turned around—their backs had been to the room at large—and glanced around. Everyone was watching the family who'd just entered. There was a gentleman, tall and handsome, with an older woman—probably his mother—on his arm. She was dressed in bombazine black with black feathers in her hair; even the gloves she wore were black. Behind them were two young women most likely only a year or two younger than Helena herself. Not only were they beauties, they were clearly twins, for Helena could not tell one from the other at all. Their identical Pomona green dresses with white embroidered shawls draped over their arms did not help the matter.

But it wasn't the lovely young ladies the room seemed to be watching with bated breath. They were watching the gentleman. Watching him, and then quickly glancing over at Helena.

She took it all back. If *this*—strange silent stares whenever a handsome man entered the room—was what she had to look forward to when venturing back into society, she would stay locked up in her room for a long time to come. Who was he anyway? Probably a rake. Nothing else made sense. If she was considered a lightskirt and he a rake, then it made sense all the guests would see them both and assume they were on the cusp of a new scandal.

The gentleman, for his part, looked as confused as Helena felt. He moved up to Lady Andrews and began speaking with their hostess. As he did so, most of the room resumed their various conversations. But Helena didn't miss that while everyone had begun speaking again, no one was truly ignoring the man.

Topper asked Emma about her thoughts on a musicale they'd both apparently attended while in London. Emma picked up the conversation with gusto and rattled on and on. Helena took the moment to carefully study the man who'd caused such a commotion by simply walking into the room.

He was tall but not overly so. He filled his jacket quite becomingly and his chestnut hair appeared as though his valet had tried to get it to set well, but the slight curl had refused to remain completely tame.

The room was beginning to feel calmer when the man walked up to Lord Forbes and greeted him.

"Chapman." Lord Forbes shook his hand, his mouth barely twitching up into a smile. "I was wondering when next I'd run into you. It's been too long."

Chapman? As in, *Lord Chapman*? The man who'd singlehandedly ruined Helena's chances at marriage? The floor seemed to tip beneath her feet, and Helena found herself grabbing Emma's arm for support. How could he be here? Of all the places he could have shown up this winter, why did it have to be here?

Lord Forbes, seemingly oblivious to all, turned their way. "This is Lady Emma," he said, even as Emma curtsied, "daughter of Lord and Lady Shakerley. They are the two standing beside the pier table, over there." Then Lord Forbes's gaze jumped over to Helena before dropping to his boots. "And this lady I'm sure you know." Then he coughed and his head came back up. "I've been dying to know, how was the hunting for you this year?"

The gentleman's brow creased, but with confusion, not anger. "I was rather too busy for any hunting. But, I beg your pardon, I do not know this young lady."

Helena felt her face grow hot, so hot she felt certain her cheeks would burn from now until she met an early grave.

Lord Forbes shifted a bit, as did the others in their small group. All except Emma.

Bless her, but she stood up straight, stuck her chin out and leveled Lord Chapman with quite the scowl.

"This is my dear friend," she said, her voice firm and commanding, "the *lovely* Miss Helena Spencer."

Lord Chapman's eyes met Helena's; they were a rich brown, soft and intelligent.

Slowly he closed his eyes and cursed softly. Though Helena would not have chosen those exact words—despite what society thought, she did strive to be a lady always—she still agreed with the sentiment.

Luckily, or perhaps Lady Andrews was concerned over what might happen if Helena and Lord Chapman spoke to one another for long, dinner was announced just then. Lord

Chapman bowed stiffly and moved off without muttering another word. The other three gentlemen shifted about, clearly unsure what to do.

Helena didn't know either. *He* was here. The one man she most despised and the one whom, she was quite certain, despised her. He'd left Town before the scandal truly broke, so he would not have felt the full weight of it as she had. He may not even be fully aware of how awful society had turned. Nonetheless, judging by his curt, well-chosen words at hearing who she was, he had heard some of it.

The whole of the room was slowly filing out the door and toward the dining room. Lord Ellis leaned forward and requested Emma walk in with him.

"Yes, thank you," she said sweetly, "and Lord Dowding—"

"Topper, I truly do insist," he said with a friendly smile. "Just Topper."

"Then, Topper, be a dear and take Miss Spencer in? Only give us a moment first."

Helena nearly balked at her friend's forwardness; at the same time she recognized as well as Emma that if someone didn't speak up for her, Helena would likely be left in the drawing room alone.

Alone again. That seemed to be the way of things now.

Both men agreed and stepped to the side so that Emma and Helena might have a moment of privacy.

"Helena, I swear, I had no idea, no notion at all that he would be here."

Helena could only nod.

"You believe me, don't you?"

Helena looked at her friend. Emma looked not only sincere, but very near crying herself. "Of course I believe you."

Emma let out a loud sigh. "Good. Then I am not completely cast down. Now, let us hurry in before—"

"No." Helena took Emma's hand in hers. "I appreciate you

securing me an escort in to dinner, but I think it best if I claim a headache and eat in my bedchamber."

Much to Helena's surprise, Emma's expression morphed, going straight from distraught penitence to stubborn determination. "There is no chance that I am going to allow you to shut yourself up again. Helena Spencer, you have let this *rumor* dictate your life for far too long. Now, turn around this instant and walk into the dining room with your chin held high."

Helena blinked. Where had this sudden insistence come from? "You cannot be serious."

"I most certainly am. You have done nothing wrong. If anyone should eat dinner alone in their room, then let it be Lord Chapman. *You* are going to enjoy this house party." Taking hold of Helena's arm, Emma all but dragged her toward Lord Ellis and Topper who patiently waited for them. "I won't allow you to cry off now," Emma hissed in Helena's ear. "I'd much rather put pepper in his after-dinner port."

"How would you do that when all the ladies will be in the drawing room?"

"I'd enlist his sisters. I can feel that they would make valuable allies if so enlisted."

"You wouldn't dare." At least, Helena hoped she wouldn't dare.

Emma shrugged. "I would if it would make you feel better." She gave Helena's arm a squeeze before disposing of her next to Topper.

Helena smiled up at the decidedly nervous gentleman. But he didn't look ready to cry off, so neither would she. More than that though, she couldn't cry off. Not utterly. She'd sent Uncle Scrooge the letter. Yes, she'd told herself that she would wait until after dinner tonight. But then Jane had found the letter and said, with a curtsy, that she'd see to getting it sent right away. Helena had almost called after her, but her abigail had disappeared too quickly. Moreover, Helena wasn't sure what excuse she would have given to explain having written and addressed a letter but not wanting to send it.

Truly, if she'd wanted to stop Jane she could have. The reality was, she *wanted* the letter sent, and as soon as possible. And she wanted her Uncle Scrooge to write back, to agree to meet her. She only wanted a family once more.

As Helena walked beside Topper into the dining room, she couldn't help but wonder if she would *ever* have a family again.

CHAPTER FOUR

The door to Fredrick's bedchamber swung open with a bang, and Christina stormed in.

"Tell Eleanor that she *cannot* have every eligible bachelor here!"

Fredrick slowly shut his eyes, lowering the book he'd been reading, and breathed in and out. Patience, he reminded himself; his sisters needed a calming influence in their lives. If he flew off the handle whenever they drove him to distraction, then he couldn't be that influence.

Trying to keep his teeth-grinding to a minimum, he turned in his chair before the fireplace and faced Christina. "Has she claimed them all, all ready?"

"Yes." Christina didn't try to hide her exasperation. "Every last one of them. Lord Ellis she says is handsome and hers. Lord Forbes she says is wealthy and hers. Topper she says is considerate—"

"And hers?"

Christina groaned loudly and flung herself down on the settee, her yellow dress pluming out and then settling around her once more.

Eleanor, in an identical yellow dress, stomped into the room. "Don't believe her. It's not true."

"It is so true!"

Fredrick rubbed at the back of his neck even as his sisters continued their heated disagreement. Before Father had passed, he'd seen a little competition between Christina and Eleanor. But immediately after the funeral, he'd caught them sitting together and comforting each other more often than not. Why they'd reverted back to being archenemies he couldn't say, but he sincerely wished back those days of quiet and peace.

It took several times of him calling both their names before either settled down enough to actually hear him. "Please, we are here for Mother, not to shackle anyone to either of you."

"Shackle?" Christina stomped her foot.

Eleanor sidled up next to Christina. "He's only saying that because he had to look at Miss Spencer all night. He's probably kicking himself now for not going through with Uncle's plan and marrying her."

Christina was quick to agree. "He always takes his dismay out on us. It isn't our fault he's such a dunderhead."

Why were they both suddenly angry at him now? Actually, it didn't matter. He'd take the anger if it meant they'd stop yelling.

"All I'm asking," he said, "is that we have a cheerful, not-dramatic Christmas. Mother needs this." Heaven knew that if it weren't for Mother, *he* would have packed his bags after seeing that Miss Spencer was included in the house party and been gone before first light.

Eleanor tipped her head up, sighing dreamily. "All I need is a gentleman like Lord Ellis vying for my hand."

Christina giggled. "Or Topper; did you see how attentive he was to Miss Spencer last night? All the while, *some people* were being rude and dismissive."

Why did she have to look at him like that? It was true; he hadn't spoken to Miss Spencer all night. But he'd felt strongly that such was the best way to quell any gossip which might spring from them both sitting down to the same table for dinner.

"A woman could *not* go wrong with a man like that," Eleanor chimed in.

Arm in arm, they began to walk back toward the bedchamber door. Just before moving out, Christina turned back around. "Aren't you coming down for breakfast?"

And risk being in the same room as Miss Spencer again? "No, thank you. I have a few correspondences I wish to answer." He knew he'd have to see her at least part of the time during the next month. But, in his opinion, the less the better.

"You're avoiding her," Eleanor said, shaking her head.

"And if I am?" he asked.

His twin sisters only shared a look, then giggled as they traipsed out the door.

What the blazes was *that* supposed to mean?

Shaking his head, Fredrick picked up his book. Between being unable to sleep for the better part of last night and not caring to leave his bedchamber this morning, he was nearly done with *Tom Jones*. He fingered the last few pages. At this rate, he'd be needing a new book before tomorrow. Perhaps he would ask Lord Andrews if he might select something new from the library down the hall from the guest rooms.

"There you are."

Or . . . he might not be finished as soon as he thought.

"Good morning, Mother," he said, lowering his book once more.

She wore all black, as she had for months now. At least this dress, with its overlays and lace, seemed more of a statement than a drudgery. He sincerely hoped she was enjoying her time with Lady Andrews—they were longstanding friends—and would continue to do so. "What can I do for you?"

"It's my bedchamber, Fred, dear. It's so frightfully drafty."

"Is it?" His own room was completely comfortable. "Does not your bed sit far away from the window?" If hers was anything like his, he couldn't imagine how she would feel a draft. His was so far away from the window, he could only just make out the imposing hedge maze in the back of the garden—a fact he was fully aware of since he hadn't risen until late that morning, on account of the guilt he felt whenever Miss Spencer's strained smile crossed his mind.

"Well, yes, but I couldn't sleep for the wind across my face. I am sure during the autumn or spring it would not be a bother at all, but in the dead of winter . . ." She left off with a shiver.

"Have you spoken to Lady Andrews?"

"Oh, no, of course not. I would hate to appear ungrateful."

"If your room is unsuitable, I am sure Lady Andrews would be more than willing to help a good friend like yourself get situated somewhere better."

Mother drew a little nearer. "I hate to bother her, especially now, when she has a house full of guests."

"Of whom you are one." Fredrick stood and took both of her hands in his. "How about I speak to Lord Andrews about it?"

"Would you? That sounds just splendid." The relief was evident in her face.

"It is no problem at all." For years, she'd had Father to do these sorts of things for her. Now, all that responsibility rested on him. He'd been shouldering it for months now, and yet, every day he wondered if he were truly doing enough.

"Come," she said, looping her arm through his. "I believe I saw Lord Andrews in the breakfast room."

She expected him to speak to Lord Andrews now? Fredrick's gaze swung to the door. "I can always find him later this morning." No doubt the man would be in his study, or the library perhaps, and would be easy enough to locate; he would also undoubtedly be far away from any of the female persuasion.

"I would feel far more at peace if you spoke with him now."

Fredrick pulled his gaze away from the door and looked at Mother. She'd aged quite a bit these last few months. The wrinkles around her eyes had deepened, and her hair sported far more gray than it had only nine months ago when they'd all gone to London for the Season—all five of them. Now, they were only four.

"Yes," Fredrick heard himself say. "Let us go down, and I will speak with him posthaste."

Fredrick allowed his mother to lead him out of his room and down the hall. The wing was a large and elaborate one, boasting of over a dozen rooms. At the end of the hallway, there were a few steps that took them down to a large landing. Directly in front of them was the family wing, off to the right the library.

Fredrick glanced over at the library; while he was speaking to Lord Andrews about his mother's room, he'd have to also ask about borrowing a book. Not that he had any concerns their host would say no to either request. Fredrick had only spoken with Lord Andrews a couple of times the night before, but he seemed a joyful, pleasing sort of man.

Fredrick and his mother turned to the left, heading down the extra-wide staircase that led to the west parlor, a grand ballroom, and the breakfast room, among other spaces in the vast house.

He led Mother down the stairs. Voices met them halfway down the hall. It seemed most of the guests had gathered in the breakfast room. Hopefully, Lord Andrews would be among them. If so, Fredrick could speak with him and have done immediately.

When he stepped through the door, his gaze instead fell on someone else—a lovely auburn-haired woman attired in a stylish, muted blue morning dress.

Miss Spencer.

Blast, but his throat grew tight just looking at her. Which he shouldn't do. At all. The less he allowed his gaze to wander her direction, the better.

Fixing his gaze on the array of food set out, Fredrick walked steadily across the room with Mother on his arm. Of all the deuced decisions he'd made since becoming Earl of Chapman, his dealings with Miss Spencer haunted him more than any other. Of course, he'd had no idea when he first sent Uncle Baker to undo all the contriving he'd done that anyone outside his own family had known of the almost-engagement. After that, he'd removed himself to the country. Yes, he'd heard rumors regarding his supposed snub of Miss Spencer; but judging by the reception the two of them had received last night at dinner, he'd left her in a far worse situation than he'd ever imagined.

"Do you not care to eat?" Mother asked in a low voice.

Fredrick blinked. They were standing before the food that filled the sideboard, and while she had a plate and several items upon it, he was only standing dumbly by.

He silenced the growl rolling about his chest—he normally wasn't this idiotic—and reached for Mother's plate. "Let me get that for you while you find a seat to your liking."

Mother handed him the plate but didn't let go right away.

Fredrick glanced up at her.

She eyed him, a peculiar expression weighing her brow down. First, Christina and Eleanor had laughed at him, and now Mother was considering him most pointedly. These were exactly the things an earl *ought* to know how to handle, yet he hadn't a notion what was to be done.

Without a word, Mother finally released the plate and strode over toward the table.

Fredrick shook his head, bending over the assortment of food, wondering what else his mother would prefer. How could a man reasonably be expected to act respectably as earl when there were so many different things always vying for his attention? He had sisters to guard and guide. He had an aging mother who needed attending. Then there was the estate—the farmers and the staff and the stewards and his father's man-of-business.

He reached for a bit of toast and added it to the plate. There were ever so many ways a man could err. He added a bit of jam to the toast. Suppose he used too heavy a hand and drove either Christina or Eleanor to do something rash? Father's friend had done that, and it very nearly ruined his family. He plopped a scoop of fruit beside the toast. Mother had confided in him that her room was too drafty, but suppose she someday decided to stop confiding in him? What would he do then? Would he even know before things grew dire? Would he know what to do if his tenants all decided to leave? If the crops all spoiled? Would he know how to care for everyone? He'd long since lost count of all the ways he could ruin his family in under six months.

He glanced down at the plate.

Gads, he'd filled it to overflowing. He couldn't serve his mother this; the rest of the guests would think she ate like a hog. Fredrick pressed two fingers against the bridge of his nose. It was barely halfway through the morning and he was already blundering.

Blessedly, no one else stood beside the sideboard. Fredrick grabbed a second plate and placed a few of Mother's favorite items on it off the overflowing plate. Let all the guests think he was a hog, but not his mother. Of course, he would probably be leaving himself open to ridicule when he took so much food and then hardly touched any of it. He'd never been much of a breakfast person.

With a plate in either hand, Fredrick turned around.

Unbidden, his gaze landed on Miss Spencer once more. He did feel sorely guilty over his dealings with her. He searched the table for Mother. Hang it all, she was sitting one chair away from Miss Spencer. The chair on her other side was filled by Lady Andrews.

Fredrick walked over to her and placed the plate with a dainty portion of food in front of Mother. But then he hesitated. If he sat, the only place left for him was between her and Miss Spencer, the latter of whom had not turned around once nor looked at him even fleetingly since he'd walked in. Not that he blamed her. It seemed they'd both come to the same conclusion: all would be best if they avoided and ignored the other.

But Fredrick couldn't remain standing. He had his own plate of food in his hand, for all to see. It's not as though he could claim disinterest in eating now. Squaring his jaw, Fredrick sat.

He could have been wrong—he didn't know Miss Spencer in the least—but he could have sworn he felt waves of resentment rolling off her. Well, he couldn't blame her for that, either.

Still, he couldn't say as much during breakfast with the whole household watching. He picked up his fork and scooped up a bit of egg. Mother spoke on about the many gifts Fredrick's father had given her during Christmas over the years. Across the table, Topper and Lord Forbes spoke in tones too soft for Fredrick to overhear, but he didn't miss that they frequently glanced his way. His and Miss Spencer's way, more specifically. A manservant moved up behind Fredrick and held out a cup of ale.

"Coffee, if you please," he replied, and the manservant moved off. Fredrick had much to see to today with an upset mother and two trouble-causing sisters; he wished to keep his wits about him.

Past Miss Spencer, Lady Emma and her parents laughed at something Christina had said. It seemed everyone at the table was joyfully engaged in conversation. That is, everyone except himself and Miss Spencer. They, alone, were silent.

It was a strange sort of connection; it was as though there was a tentative link between them, their own displeasure at being together somehow uniting them.

The manservant returned with a mug of coffee and placed it on the table. Fredrick thanked the man but couldn't focus on anything but the beautiful, wary woman at his side. Unity in mutual aversion? What rot. The trip here must have worn him out more than he had originally thought. He leaned over to his left, angling toward Mother and decidedly away from Miss Spencer. They may have to reside in the same house for the next several weeks, but he'd be hanged if that meant he had to talk to her.

After a few minutes of nodding and smiling, however, Fredrick realized he was far too distracted to follow whatever conversation his mother and Lady Andrews were having. It didn't matter, either way. He was only here until he'd faked enough interest in breakfast to excuse himself and go find Lord Andrews.

Reaching for his coffee, Fredrick continued to feign interest in what his hostess was saying. He gave the cup a slow stir and lifted it to his lips.

The liquid was hot, and . . . Lud!

Fredrick choked on the drink and more than a little trailed down his jacket as he sat up with a jolt.

What in the blazes?

All the table was watching him. He shook his hand and felt

droplets of coffee spray his cheek. Pulling out his handkerchief he pressed it to his mouth even as he glared at his coffee mug. What was in there? Coffee, yes, but something else, to be sure. The flavor was vaguely familiar, but he couldn't place it. He set the mug down and stood. The room was silent.

Pepper. That's what it was. A huge amount of pepper had been added to his coffee. Fredrick glanced about, his gaze, as it had many times already that morning, landing on Miss Spencer. She *still* was not looking at him. Nonetheless, he detected a nearly hidden, smug smile pulling at the corner of her lips.

What a troublesome woman. Fredrick drew himself up and addressed the room at large. "How clumsy of me." He bowed shallowly, trying to calm the tightness of his throat and a loud cough. "Please excuse me." At least now he had a perfectly sound reason to leave the breakfast room.

He rounded the table and reached the door in only a few long strides. He couldn't help but glance back though, just before passing through.

Miss Spencer was finally looking at him. And yes, that was most certainly a smile across her face. It would seem that his refusal to Baker's plan had been quite the blessing.

He may not know her well, but he now knew Miss Spencer to be a very vexing woman, indeed.

CHAPTER FIVE

*H*elena slowly sat atop the wide and luxurious bed. The room about her was dark, with only a bit of space around the fireplace and a much smaller pool about the candle in her hand lit by a soft fire's glow. Holding the cream-colored candle in both her hands, Helena focused on the cold floor beneath her feet and the comforting softness on which she sat.

Nighttime was always the hardest.

During the day, she could smile joyfully, she could laugh, she could even think up a bit of wit now and then. She could go so far as to even convince herself that all was well.

But, inevitably night fell. The sun disappeared and heavy darkness encompassed even the best lit parlors and card tables. Eventually, she always had to retire to her bedchamber, where she was alone. *Dreadfully* alone.

In the silence and the blackness, there were no distractions, no company to draw her attention, nothing to hide behind.

There was only the truth.

And the truth was, Helena was horribly afraid.

She'd always struggled to fall asleep, even as a young girl.

Of course, then it was far more simple worries that kept her up: would her head cold clear in time to go ice skating on Christmas day? Would her father return from his most recent trip whole and healthy? Would Emma find the courage to perform at the next musicale?

Now, however, the worries had deepened, intensifying into near panic. Suppose she was unable to attain an offer of marriage? Suppose the scandal of earlier that year followed her the rest of her life? Suppose she was destined to always fall asleep alone?

Helena shook her head. She firmly believed that fretting over an issue never did anyone any good. Still, that didn't entail it was easy to brush off her concerns come night.

Her day had proven particularly trying, which didn't help matters. Though most of the guests were polite when she was present, she'd noticed more than one conversation end abruptly when she entered a room. Several of the ladies sat down to cards that afternoon, only to feign fatigue once she showed interest in joining. Topper had been attentive and kind, but all other gentlemen had seemed less than eager to be seen beside her when everyone had dressed warmly for a quick turn about the snow-covered gardens.

Slowly, Helena sat the candle down on the table beside her bed and slipped between the bedclothes. Emma had insisted she had a plan which would make everything right. The idea both comforted and alarmed Helena; it was sweet of her to worry, but what could she possibly do for Helena? Placing pepper in Lord Chapman's coffee that morning *had* been most diverting. Truly as satisfying as Emma had predicted. But as the day had worn on—and worn on *her*—even the memory of his shocked expression could not lighten her mood.

She would simply close her eyes and allow herself to drift into oblivion. Or perhaps distract herself with memories of the Royal Menagerie. She could still clearly recall the mesmerizing sound of monkeys chattering, the awe-inspiring chills she felt at hearing the lion roar, the thrill of being stared down by the glassy black eyes of the leopard.

Once the morning light peeked through the curtains of her room, she would find her positivity again. She would laugh and smile at eligible bachelors. Helena squeezed her eyes shut. This would pass. She needn't worry. Certainly someday, she would meet a gentleman who would come up to scratch; there were several very fine gentlemen in attendance this Christmas.

But suppose not one of them cared for her?

Helena's stomach clenched up in an anxious twist.

She set her jaw and tried to focus on relaxing her legs and arms. She was drifting on a cloud . . . not a worry or a care . . . nothing weighing her down . . .

Excepting there was a very real chance she would not be welcomed at very many assemblies next Season. Every year after that, she'd be invited less and less often to outings and gatherings. When society turned their collective backs on someone, it could be most condemning.

She groaned and rolled onto her side. So much for being light as a cloud.

With a grunt, Helena sat up. This was ridiculous. Lying back down, she placed her pillow *atop* her head instead of beneath it, blocking out the last, lingering bits of light in the room.

She would sleep.

She was determined.

Her worries and fears could go and hang themselves for all she cared.

Though the minutes stretched, eventually she did succumb to the elusive call of sleep. But her fears did not leave her at the threshold between consciousness and oblivion.

Helena stood with a bright red shawl wrapped about her shoulders. Slowly she turned about. She was in a dark maze with tall hedges for walls and a path overgrown with knee-high grass. Though she could see no more than a few feet in front of her, she could sense the vastness of the maze, the intricate way the path weaved around and around itself.

She walked forward, immediately coming upon her first decision. Right or straight? Stars hung in the night sky above her, as did a large yellow moon, but none of the celestial orbs gave her any indication which way she should choose. Helena chose to turn right. She had to lift her legs rather high just to get them through the tall grass.

Someone screamed; that sounded like Emma. Helena twisted about, her skirt catching in the grass and refusing to turn with her. It tightened about her thighs, nearly tripping her.

A dark shadow slipped over the path she'd just crossed. A cold wind tripped down her spine. Even as she watched, the shadow grew, filling the path.

It reached out.

It lunged for her—

Helena sat up in bed.

The bedposts were the only things standing over her, the blankets the only things around her legs. She breathed heavily and slowly closed her eyes, tipping her head back.

It had only been another nightmare. *Stupid dreams.* She'd thought she'd grown out of them. Helena ran a few fingers over her forehead. Her hand was shaking.

She glanced over at the small candle, burning much lower now. She should have extinguished it before falling asleep earlier, but now she was grateful she hadn't thought to do so. The light was small, but it brought a bit of comfort.

Willing her breath to calm, she searched about for her pillow and found it on the floor. It must have tumbled off the bed when she awoke with a start. Helena picked it up, fluffed it, and then placed the pillow back where it belonged. Resting back against its softness, she kept her gaze trained on the flickering candlelight. When she was very young and one of her nightmares struck, she would slip into bed with her father. They'd always been close. Never once had Father been upset at Helena for waking him up in the middle of the night. Instead, he'd always allowed Helena some space beside him.

But now Father was gone, resting beside his wife, beside Helena's dear mother. He would never again be there to comfort her. The pulsing pain of loss filled Helena's chest, poignant and strong. She hadn't cried over her parents for weeks, yet suddenly, her eyes burned and tears fell down her cheeks.

Helena blinked, the sight of the candle still blurred. All she could do was watch the tiny bit of light and grieve for the joyful times that she feared might never come again.

CHAPTER SIX

Fredrick's attention was split.

On the one hand, Christina and Eleanor were standing near the back of the room, engaged in an animated, if quite hushed, conversation with Lady Emma. They'd had no previous connection with Lady Emma, so why his sisters were suddenly so rapt by what she had to say, he could not fathom. It bothered him. Something about the way they huddled close, their shoulders nearly touching, clearly indicated they did not want to be disturbed. It could only portend trouble. Fredrick fidgeted in his seat; no doubt, whatever trouble his sisters were involved in, he would be left to remedy.

He would have to speak with them later. For now, he truly ought to be paying more attention to Miss Wynn on the pianoforte. After all, Lady Andrews had insisted he not disappear immediately after dinner tonight, as he'd done these past few evenings.

Neither his gaze nor his thoughts remained on Miss Wynn for long. Because, on the other hand, Miss Spencer sat alone on the row of seats in front of him, far to his left. She had not been sitting by herself for most of the night; Lady Emma had been by her side. But since her friend had left, Fredrick had a clear line of sight to her.

And she looked terrible.

Had she not slept well the night before? There were dark circles about her eyes and her shoulders slumped slightly. He thought back quickly to breakfast—he hadn't seen her there—and then on to cards that afternoon. She'd been sitting on the opposite side of the room, so he hadn't noticed if she was acting worn thin or not. He sincerely hoped she was all right. Theirs may be a complicated past, but he wished her all the best. Miss Spencer's lips pulled into a tired frown. Fredrick's stomach tightened at the sight. She certainly did not appear to be enjoying 'all the best.'

Clapping erupted around him, nearly making Fredrick start. Blast, he'd been so busy woolgathering he'd all but forgotten the performance taking place. Fredrick lifted his hands and clapped as well. Miss Wynn stood and smiled sweetly. She curtsied and then curtsied again at the rigorous applause.

"Miss Spencer," Lady Andrews called from the other side of the room, "we have not heard you play at all this Christmas. Would you care to indulge us?"

It seemed everyone in the room turned toward her as one. Fredrick kept his gaze down but could not deny his curiosity. How would she react, this woman who'd slipped pepper into his coffee, yet dressed quite plainly?

She was silent for a moment before stating clearly, "Thank you, but no. I cannot claim much talent on the pianoforte."

He was sorry to hear it; he'd rather have liked to hear her play.

"However," she continued, "if you have a harp, I wouldn't mind performing on that instrument."

"How unfortunate." Lady Andrews's words were tight, though she didn't sound like she was apologizing. "We have the pianoforte and a guitar, but the only harp is currently stored in the attic." She waved a hand toward the room's ceiling. "Much too out of the way to be brought down. No one has bothered to play the instrument in decades."

"I see," Miss Spencer said.

"Lady Andrews is right," Miss Wynn chimed in. "We all want for another song and if you will not, Miss Spencer, then I propose that *you* choose who shall play next."

If Miss Spencer was surprised by the strange demand, she did not show it. "You will forgive me, but I do not know those in attendance well enough to know who would suit." Her eyes flitted quickly over to her friend, Lady Emma, who was still standing in the back beside Fredrick's sisters.

Fredrick's gaze followed hers. Lady Emma had her head down, but she looked as though she had grown pale.

"Do you not?" Miss Wynn's statement sounded increasingly like a challenge. Though her voice grew quiet, no one in the silent room was likely to miss her next statement. "I suppose you do not often associate with those of the *haut ton* anymore, do you?"

Fredrick eyed the individuals around him. He'd noticed a palpable discomfort the first night both he and Miss Spencer were in the drawing room together, waiting to go into dinner. But after that, he thought everyone as a whole had decided to ignore whatever had happened during the Season. Apparently, he had been wrong.

"Well," Lady Andrews said, "if you are not so inclined, perhaps . . ." She waved a hand toward Lady Emma.

Before Lady Andrews could say more, Miss Spencer stood suddenly. "If you insist, I could play something simple."

Miss Wynn smirked while Lady Andrews only stared, clearly surprised.

"Well, all right, then," she stammered.

Miss Spencer glanced once more at her friend. Fredrick

followed suit just in time to catch sight of Lady Emma's silent "thank you" before Miss Spencer moved to the front and sat at the instrument.

The room stilled as the first few notes filled the air. Most attention was lost, though, after only a few lines. When Miss Spencer had said she was not accomplished, she had not been falsely modest. Soon, those around him began softly spoken conversations. Miss Spencer's song ended quickly, and the applause was meager compared to what Miss Wynn had received. Nonetheless, Fredrick found it hard to put the performance from his mind. Not during the rest of the night's various conversations, not as the group dispersed to retire, and not as he climbed the stairs and made his way to his bedchamber.

Miss Spencer clearly did not care to perform on the pianoforte—nor was she proficient—yet she had not hesitated to stand up so that her friend would not have to. And Lady Emma had been noticeably grateful.

Fredrick shut the door behind himself and tugged on his cravat. Her actions intrigued him, and he couldn't help but respect her for it.

A knock sounded at his bedchamber door.

Who could that be? Fredrick turned and opened the door a slit.

Eleanor stood in the corridor. "Oh good; you're not dressed for bed yet."

"How could I be? There hasn't been time."

"Never mind that. Christina and I need your help."

When did they *not* need his help with something? "Come morning, we can talk and I'm sure we can find—"

"No," Eleanor whispered-yelled. "We need you to come *now*."

A wave of exhaustion washed over him. He placed a hand against the door frame and pressed his forehead against it. "Must it be tonight?"

"Of course. We might be seen if we did this during the day."

Ah, lud. This sounded like the trouble he'd been expecting. He could just push Eleanor and Christina—wherever his other sister may be at the moment—away, telling them he'd deal with their problem later. But Fredrick knew from harsh experience that they'd probably just go ahead with their plan *without* him, and that would inevitably make matters far worse.

"Fine." He finished pulling off the limp cravat from around his neck and tossed it onto a nearby chair. "What have you two gotten yourselves into this time?"

Eleanor took his hand in both of hers, pulling him down the corridor. "Just come and see."

"Oh, sit down already," Emma said.

Helena groaned and plopped down onto the iron bench in the orangery. "But why are we here? In the middle of the night?"

"And stop asking so many questions."

"Very *reasonable* questions."

Footsteps echoed from behind Helena.

"There you are," Emma said, addressing the newcomer.

Helena twisted on the bench. It was Lady Eleanor—or Lady Christina. Helena still struggled to tell the twins apart. Surely Lord Chapman knew the secret of which was Lady Christina, and which was Lady Eleanor. It was rather a shame they hadn't the type of relationship that permitted her to ask him.

"Where's your sister?" Emma asked.

"Eleanor had something to see to. But don't worry; she'll be here shortly."

So this was Lady Christina. Well, that was one mystery

solved, but it did absolutely nothing to help her understand why Emma had asked her here. She probably would have said no, except she had not been looking forward to the darkness and solitude of her room. It was childish, but she hadn't been able to dislodge the dread her nightmare had brought all day.

Lady Christina sat on the small bench beside her. "How are you?" she said to Helena. "I am certain I would have cried most ardently had Miss Wynn said such horrid things about *me*. I'd rather thought she'd gotten it all out of her system earlier today during cards."

Helena lifted a single brow. If Miss Wynn's comments during the spontaneous musicale were only a snippet of what the woman had been saying to all and sundry, Helena was more than glad she had paid the woman so little attention and had declined to sit with her at cards that afternoon.

"If Miss Wynn, or anyone, is speaking ill of me, don't bother to enlighten me." When her broken near-engagement had become known and the rumors had first begun, Helena had, naturally, been curious as to what was being said about her. Emma had only had to report a few overheard statements before Helena wised up and stopped asking. Soon, however, she couldn't have ignored the slights even if she'd wanted to. By now, she was thoroughly fed up with rumors. Let people say what they would; she didn't care to hear about it.

"You are so brave," Lady Christina said with a sigh.

Helena studied the young woman beside her—her wide brown eyes, perfectly curled hair, and fashionable dress. Not many years ago, she'd been like this young woman. Eager to enter society. Excited to see the sights, to *breathe* in all that was diverting.

Then, Father had passed.

Then, she'd almost become engaged.

Then, society had deemed her unfit.

Suddenly, Helena didn't feel brave. She simply felt old.

More footsteps sounded from behind her. Lady Eleanor, no doubt. Helena waited, except Emma's face didn't show pleasure. She stared at the newcomer, her eyes slightly wider than was natural. Helena once more twisted about on the bench.

It was Lady Eleanor, but beside her was Lord Chapman.

Helena felt the same crawl of doubt and apprehension across her chest that she experienced whenever he walked into the room. Though she wanted nothing more than an excuse to ignore him—they both were becoming quite good at doing just that—she couldn't seem to look away, either. He was still attired in his evening dress, except his jacket hung unbuttoned and open and his cravat was missing completely. The combination highlighted how well he filled his jacket. It also brought a lick of heat to Helena's cheeks. How had *he* ended up here?

Lord Chapman seemed to collect himself quicker than she was able. He pulled his gaze away from her and instead stared down his sisters. "Christina." His voice was every bit as ominous as his glare. "Eleanor. I will have an explanation."

Neither sister seemed to give his displeasure a passing care. Lady Christina quickly stood. "Thanks for bringing him," she said to her twin. "Now we can begin."

Each sister took one of his arms and all but dragged him over to the bench, depositing him directly beside Helena.

She scooted as far away as the small piece of furniture would allow. He did the same, pushing himself up against the opposite side. Helena looked up at Emma and leveled her own black look in her friend's direction.

Emma squirmed a bit and had the audacity to look unsure and apologetic. "Excuse me, Lady Christina, Lady Eleanor," she said, "But I had not thought . . ." She motioned toward Lord Chapman.

"We need a man's perspective," one of the twins said. Helena had already lost track of which was which. Hadn't anyone ever told them they ought not to dress the same?

"He can be our informer," the other added.

"This is Fredrick's fault anyway. He ought to take part in remedying it."

"No one would suspect *him* of helping Miss Spencer. It's perfect."

If Helena had any questions regarding the color of her face before, she was certain it was red now. "I don't need Lord Chapman's help with anything, thank you."

The sisters shook their heads in unison. "You don't even know of the plan yet," one said.

Helena didn't need to know; even her nightmares were starting to not sound too bad in comparison to this. Helena made to stand, but Emma stopped her with a hand on her shoulder.

"Helena." At some point since Lord Chapman had entered the orangery, Emma had left her uncertainty behind and was taking charge once again. "I insist you stay and hear us out."

Helena sat back down. "Then speak quickly. It's late and I wish to be done with today."

"Hear, hear," Lord Chapman said too softly for anyone but her to notice.

Whatever Emma and the two sisters had cooked up, Lord Chapman was clearly as unwilling an accomplice as she was.

"Helena," Emma said, drawing herself up, "it's time you face the truth. Because of the"—she eyed Lord Chapman—"happenings of last Season, you are quickly being relegated to the shelf."

More like *shoved* onto the shelf.

"It has become clear that with each passing month, the chances of you making a match are diminishing."

"Please," Helena said, dryly, "don't bother sugarcoating it just for me."

Emma puffed out a sigh of exasperation. "I'm sorry, but facts are facts."

That may very well be true, but it wasn't as though Emma was enlightening her of anything she didn't already know. "Why are we here, Emma?"

"We have decided . . ." Emma paused as Lady Christina and Lady Eleanor scooted over beside her, making it clear who "we" included, "that this Christmas, we are going to find you a husband."

Helena's jaw dropped open before she could stop it. "A what?"

"And Fredrick is going to help us," one of the sisters said, not bothering to answer Helena.

"Excuse me?" he asked.

"It's exquisite," the other twin said. "There are ever so many eligible gentlemen present. One is sure to come up to scratch if only we apply ourselves."

Lord Chapman stood. "Out of the question. I specifically said we were to have no drama this winter season."

"You said we aren't here to shackle a man to one of *us*," the other twin said, "but that isn't what we are trying to do."

They were here to "shackle" someone to Helena. Grand.

Emma looped her arm through one of the sister's, also staring Lord Chapman down. "This *is* your fault, you realize. I believe that, as a gentleman, you should not deny an opportunity to make things right."

Helena's head swam. As the three women standing before her argued with Lord Chapman, all she could do was put her head in her hands and ignore them.

Purposely chase down a man? Connive and contrive and all but beg to be wed? Who would ever agree to such a thing? She'd always imagined marrying a man for whom she cared, someone she, at the very least, respected. Then again, Emma was correct. She was beginning to realize that the longer she took, the harder it would be to prove herself worthy of high society. And the gentlemen here at Lady Andrews's house party did all seem quite upstanding.

"Miss Spencer." Helena looked up at Lord Chapman's address. His hands were clasped behind his back, and he faced her fully.

"Your friend and my sisters make a valid point. Your situation is regrettable, and I am partially to blame."

"Neither you nor I am to blame, sir." Her voice sounded about as firm as melting snow and she couldn't seem to ignore the hazy tingling spreading across her head, blocking out reasonable thought.

"Be that as it may, I would be honored to help you regain your good standing."

Helena slowly stood, her gaze moving from him, to his sisters, and then on to Emma. She wanted to be polite, but the exhaustion of the day was heavy on her shoulders.

"While I am sensible to the generosity of your offer, I truly wish to simply let things lie. Emma, I promised you I wouldn't cry off, and I won't. Only, allow me to enjoy this Christmas, please, without worrying and fretting over what has been."

Emma stepped forward and took hold of Helena's hands in her own. "I wish I could. I wish more than anything you could simply prove to those in attendance that you are all that is good and lovely and that would prove the end of the rumors. But even if you convince those in attendance, once this house party ends, you will be right back to where you were before." Emma squeezed her hands, and it had the strange effect of nearly squeezing a few tears out of Helena's eyes. "I want you to be happy. Not only this Christmas but always."

Helena looked past her friend at the other three. Both Lady Christina and Lady Eleanor looked sincerely willing to help her; they'd both impressed her these past few days with their sincerity and kindness. Then there was Lord Chapman. What must he be thinking? His gaze met hers. His look was a soft one — his dark brown eyes conveying both an apology for putting her in this situation and a genuine desire to help set things right. He, too, these past days, had impressed her with his sincerity and kindness. It seemed those traits ran strong in his family.

Still, asking them all to help her persuade a man to marry her? Was this truly what she wished for?

Then again, the alternative was likely a life of solitary days and lonely nights. Didn't she want a family again?

"Very well, then," she heard herself say. "I agree. Let's find me a husband."

CHAPTER SEVEN

Fredrick could only stare at himself in the mirror as his valet carefully crafted the perfect cravat. Had he really agreed to help find Miss Spencer a husband? The very woman he'd declined to marry himself? Gads, but a man could be compelled to do nearly anything when three headstrong women accosted him. That had been the night before last—Lady Emma had claimed she needed a day to strategize before they began in earnest. As of yet, nothing had come from his accession, but he knew the clock was ticking, and soon he would have to make good on the agreement.

Once dressed, Fredrick made his way out of the bedchamber door and slowly down the corridor. Lady Andrews had mentioned cards this afternoon, and Mother had mentioned, in a none too vague manner, that she expected him to join her. It wasn't that he disliked cards, and he certainly didn't dislike his mother's company, but those few days holed up in his bedchamber *had* proved a nice respite. Now that he had no reason to avoid Miss Spencer and every reason to be out in company, he already missed his time of solitude.

"Don't you look fine today," Eleanor said, stepping out of her room and looping her arm through his.

"As do you," he replied. He was glad she wore white today, trimmed in pink. Though he would never say as much out loud, seeing his mother and sisters all attired in matte black had only made mourning more dismal. He had no intention to press Mother to return to more colorful clothing, but he was relieved that at least his sisters were done with mourning and could dress in something other than black.

"Between you and me," she whispered, "I believe I look far superior in white than Christina."

Fredrick chuckled. "You realize most people can't even tell you two apart." Especially considering how they nearly always insisted on wearing the exact same dress.

"They may not be able to tell from day-to-day. But in the moment, I am certain I appear at the greater advantage dressed in white."

"If you say so."

"You know," Eleanor tugged on Fredrick's arm, pulling him to a stop, "while we are about the matchmaking business for Miss Spencer, we could always broaden our efforts to include you as well."

Fredrick blanched. "No, thank you."

"I'm serious. We all agree it's about time."

"Who's 'we'?" He was nearly afraid to ask.

"Mother, Christina . . . a few of our closer friends."

Oh, lud. "I ask that you would refrain from speaking of my much-anticipated demise with *anyone* outside our immediate family." He would ask his sisters and mother to stop speaking of it even amongst themselves, but he knew a futile request when he heard it.

"Demise? Must you always use such depressing words to describe marriage?"

"I'm serious, Eleanor. Besides, I absolutely cannot consider making a connection this Christmas."

"I don't see why not."

He pinned her with a stare; he needed her to understand in no uncertain terms; anything less and he ran the risk of her doing something insane behind his back. "Because of Miss Spencer. How would it look if I were to suddenly become engaged at the very house party where my one-time-almost-intended was present? Think of the slight that would be."

For Eleanor's part, she did look appropriately humbled. "I see. That would be awful."

"What would be awful?"

Fredrick and Eleanor turned. Lady Emma was only a few paces away and closing the distance quickly.

"Ah, nothing," Fredrick quickly said before Eleanor could try to explain; no doubt, that would have led to a very awkward conversation. "We were on our way down to cards. Care to join us?" That sounded like a natural change of topic. He only hoped it would stick.

"Yes, I was headed that way as well, only . . ." She paused, glancing about the corridor. "I thought Helena was waiting for me here in the corridor. She was ready before I was but said she would wait so we could walk down together."

"Perhaps she chose to go down and meet you in the drawing room?" Eleanor offered.

Lady Emma began to nod, but then her brow creased. "I must admit, I doubt she would have."

"I shall go check," Eleanor said, already moving away. "If she is with the others, I will come back and let you know."

"Thank you," Lady Emma called after her.

Fredrick took a step forward. "I shall go as well and—"

"Actually," Lady Emma interrupted, "I was hoping to speak with you in private."

He stopped, but remained silent, watching her warily. Last

time he'd had a semi-private conversation with Lady Emma, he had been guilted into something he never would have agreed to in regular circumstances. Come to think of it, the only interaction he'd had with a Shakerley before today had been when her father had written up a contract for Fredrick to wed Helena without either of their say-so, without either of them having even met first. He was right not to trust a private conversation with anyone in the family.

"I have spent a great deal of time watching all the eligible bachelors present. I believe Lord Ellis, Topper, or Lord Forbes would each make a fine husband for Helena."

In the back of his mind, the realization that Lady Emma hadn't grouped *him* in the eligible bachelor category nagged at him a bit; was he not considered eligible? He'd always thought himself a fine gentleman. Then again, she was considering prospective husbands *for Miss Spencer*, which he certainly was not.

"That sounds like a fine list," he said. "Surely one of them will take a liking to Miss Spencer. She is . . . I mean to say, she . . ."

Lady Emma folded her arms tightly against her. "My friend is *what*, exactly?"

Miss Spencer was . . . well, he couldn't rightly say. She was pleasing enough to look at, he supposed, in the high-collared, muted dresses she seemed to prefer. But he couldn't say what kind of a conversationalist she was since they'd still had yet to truly have one.

"She is high-spirited," he finally said.

Lady Emma's stiff posture fell away, and she leaned in, almost eagerly. "When have you ever seen her act thusly?" Her question was not mocking, but sincere.

"Well . . ." Pepper in his coffee came quickly to mind.

"Don't misunderstand," Lady Emma hurried on, "I agree. Only, she hasn't been nearly as vivacious since her father passed." Her expression turned sad. "I dearly miss who she was before."

Fredrick's heart ached a bit for Miss Spencer. He could relate to the pain of losing a beloved parent. He understood all too well how it changed one, how it took the joy out of life.

A door opened and he turned toward the sound. Miss Spencer slipped into the corridor and over toward him and Lady Emma. Except—

She certainly wasn't wearing any high-collared, muted dress now. Instead, she was attired in mint green; a white ribbon showcased her slim waist, and a matching one in her hair brought out the softness of her curls. Freckles covered her nose and cheeks. Why did auburn-haired women always freckle more than anyone else he knew? Regardless, though society most likely turned their noses up at the so-called 'imperfections,' Fredrick found them quite endearing on Miss Spencer. They continued down her cheeks, neck, and past her collar bone—which was bare for the first time ever. Her neckline was not scandalously low, not by any means, but neither was it the high, overly decorous collar he'd seen her wear thus far. The dress, on the whole, fit her well, outlining the curves he'd not realized she had before now.

"Helena Spencer." Lady Emma's tone was scolding. "What do you think you are about?"

"Since you insist on finding me a husband, I wish him to be a man who likes *me*, and this is how I care to dress."

"Nonsense. You know why that dress is a bad idea."

Fredrick couldn't see *anything* wrong with how Miss Spencer looked, so he kept his mouth shut and let the two women have it out.

"I won't marry a man who believes I only care for staid, bland dresses. Suppose I am then stuck wearing them for the rest of my life?"

"After you're married, no man will care how you dress."

Fredrick didn't fully agree; if he had a wife who looked like Miss Spencer did now, he'd very much want her to dress just like that as often as possible.

"Moreover," Miss Spencer pressed on, "I only wore those stuffy dresses to avoid gossip. Clearly, that hasn't worked out. So why continue?"

Lady Emma turned toward him suddenly. "Your sisters insisted that a man's perspective would be helpful. So then, tell us, is Helena more likely to make an *honorable* match dressed like this? Or as she has been dressing?"

He had been hoping they wouldn't ask his opinion. He should have known better.

"I can see why you asked Miss Spencer to dress . . ." His instincts told him 'boring' and 'stale' were not words he should use right now, so he searched his mind for something else. ". . . with such dignity." Neither woman seemed upset by that word, so Fredrick hurried on before they changed their minds. "But I agree with Miss Spencer. She should dress in a manner true to herself. It will help her catch the eye of her most promising suitor."

Lady Emma pursed her lips. "Is that so?"

"I believe so." Plus, Miss Spencer looked stunning. He almost wished he could tell her as much, but given their complicated past, he couldn't see such a compliment as being anything but awkward. Nonetheless, though it may be a demeaning commentary on his own sex, there was no doubt in his mind that she was *far* more likely to attract a gentleman's attention—dishonorable and honorable alike—when she dressed as she was now.

Lady Emma didn't have an immediate reply, but neither did she argue.

"It's settled then." Miss Spencer was apparently ready to claim her friend's silence as surrender. "Let us go down and join the party." With that, Miss Spencer placed her hand atop Fredrick's arm.

Heat blossomed where her hand touched him. Fredrick became instantly aware of how close she stood beside him, of her skirt brushing against his leg. It was only due to years of walking with his sisters and mother that allowed him to act out of instinct and begin walking down the corridor. Lady Emma took his other arm. It was a most natural thing to do, as they were all headed the same direction and, as the gentleman present, it was expected he would see them delivered safely to the drawing room. And yet Lady Emma's presence was hardly worth noting for how aware he was of Miss Spencer.

He shouldn't be so flustered by Miss Spencer's touch. Had he not walked beside any number of other women during countless occasions?

Why then, did his whole world suddenly feel as though it was spinning?

HELENA KNEW THE MINUTE SHE'D SLIPPED AWAY FROM EMMA and decided to change into the mint green dress that her decision would draw attention. She just hadn't fathomed *how much* attention. On Lord Chapman's arm, she entered the drawing room along with Emma. At first, barely a glance was cast their way. But then, first one guest then another stopped and stared, much as Lord Chapman had when she'd first left her bedchamber. She should have known then that her decision would have such a consequence.

Keeping her gaze up—she was never one to cower under scrutiny—she left Lord Chapman's side and glided as elegantly as she could manage over to Lady Andrews. They greeted one another and then talked for a few minutes before Lady Andrews excused herself. By then, at least, no one was still watching her, though Helena caught a few quick glances her way. As Lady Andrews left, Lady Shakerley stepped up beside Helena.

"Good show, dear girl," she whispered low. "I only wish I'd been there to see Emma's face when you came walking out looking so breathtaking."

Helena smiled. "She gave me an ear full."

"I don't doubt it."

"Never you mind though because I gave it right back."

Lady Shakerley laughed. "Then I'm doubly sorry I missed out. Now," she draped an arm protectively across Helena's shoulders, "don't you mind Miss Wynn or anyone else. You just focus on being the beautiful, confident woman your father raised you to be."

A small wave of sorrow rose up at the mention of her Father. Graciously, it was not overwhelming this time. Thankful she'd found a friend in Lady Shakerley, even more so since her father had passed, Helena drew herself up, blinked a few times, and nodded her agreement. He had raised her to not hide in corners or sit silently by as others controlled the conversation.

As the afternoon rolled on, Helena visited with Lady Eleanor, Lord Forbes, and Lord Andrews, then she spoke with Lord Ellis, and Lord and Lady Shakerley. During a conversation with Lady Andrews, Helena learned that the house's name, Hedgewood Manor, was appropriately reflected in the large hedge maze spanning the grounds to the South. However, the knowledge of whether or not the maze was first and then the house named to match, or the house named and then the hedge maze grown to match was lost to history.

At one point during the day, Helena even took a small turn about the room with Miss Wynn; though their conversation was a bit stilted, they got along well enough. Perhaps Emma had been more right about Helena coming for Christmas than even she'd realized. In Town, one was always meeting new people. While that had its advantages, for one with an undeserved reputation, like Helena, it also had its disadvantages. But here, at least she was in company with the same people enough that they had no choice but to begin to see past the rumors—or so she hoped. Only time would tell.

Lady Andrews was droning on about how unpatriotic it was for her neighbor to set napkins—*French* napkins—at the supper table during a ball several months prior when Helena heard Emma call her name. She made a quick apology and slipped away. It wasn't that she supported France, far from it, but she'd heard the argument against using napkins enough times for it to have become tedious. Now, if someone could figure out how to end the war and bring their soldiers home, then she would be quite riveted.

Helena reached Emma's side, but before she could say anything, her friend took hold of her arm, just above the wrist. It wasn't an iron-grip hold, but it clearly signified that Helena wasn't getting away until Emma's purpose had been revealed.

Without a word to her, Emma only turned back to those around the card table. "I am so sorry, but I have a dreadful headache coming on. I simply cannot stay and finish the hand."

Lord Chapman and one of his sisters—one of these days Helena *would* learn how to tell the difference—sat on either side of Emma, clearly partnering in their game. Across from Helena was Topper. Emma gave none of them time to respond.

"I know it's unforgivable to cry off in the middle of the game and leave you all in the lurch, but I am sure Helena would not mind taking my place at the table. She is much wittier than I and will prove a better partner for you, Topper, I am sure."

So *this* was why Emma had called her over—to force Topper to partner with her. Helena wasn't sure if she should feel bothered with her friend, or simply thankful. Topper had proven himself to be a considerate gentleman on more than one occasion.

Emma stood and so did both gentlemen. "I think I just need a bit of a rest before dinner."

It was probably best if Helena didn't bother to argue. Topper expressed his concern over Emma's headache but also agreed to partner with Helena for the rest of the game.

Helena slipped into the chair across from him and picked up her cards. It was time she began searching for a husband in earnest.

Playing a high numbered card, she faced Topper fully. "Tell me, sir," she began, "have you ever visited the Royal Menagerie?"

CHAPTER EIGHT

Helena had spent the better part of the past two hours conversing with Lord Forbes. Though he'd been an agreeable enough partner, Helena felt tired and drawn out. She'd forced herself to smile and carry on during her card game with Topper that afternoon. Then she'd conversed with Lord Ellis during dinner and well past the time when her back had begun to ache and her eyes were feeling heavy. After withdrawing and leaving the men to their port, Helena had almost excused herself, but an ardent shake of the head from Emma had stopped her. When the men had finally joined them, Lord Forbes had been last to enter the room and had taken the only remaining available seat—which Helena was certain was the only reason he'd sat next to her.

As soon as Lady Andrews had excused herself, Helena had followed suit. She had no misconceptions over her aim—she both wanted and intently needed a good match, but that didn't necessitate she find love.

Love was better suited to younger women than her. Women who had fathers to root out money-diggers. Women who had mothers to introduce them to the best sorts of families and young men. As a woman who was nearly on the shelf, who had neither mother nor father, and who didn't have the means financially to care for herself if ever the Shakerleys grew tired of her company, Helena was not a woman who could wait for love.

It was just as well. In her experience—at least those that she'd observed in her friends and acquaintances—hearts were rather fickle things.

Helena reached the bottom of the stairs. The great entryway was empty, save her, and was so quiet she could hear the soft voices of the other guests still entertaining themselves in the parlor. She could also hear the clink of dishes from the back of the house. No doubt, this large a house party made enough dishes and laundry to keep any scullery maid busy from dawn to dusk.

The clinking paused momentarily and then was followed by the most enormous crash. Helena paused with one foot on the lowest stair. Good heavens, but that had sounded destructive. Angry shouts floated up from the direction of the kitchen, growing closer the longer Helena listened.

Curious, she moved back into the entryway. She'd seen the staff at Hedgewood Manor act in nothing short of the most proper ways. That she could hear yelling now was quite out of the ordinary.

A little girl tore into the entryway. She was watching behind herself and not where she was going and ran directly into Helena.

With a shriek, the little girl jumped to the side and tried to dart around her, but Helena caught her with a hand on her arm.

"Just what is the meaning of this?" Helena asked, unable to hide the bit of laughter that pushed through her words.

The little girl looked up. Her eyes were wide and filled with tears. The sight tore at Helena's heart. Such an expression of terror she'd never before beheld. That it came from someone so young was heartbreaking.

"Mary!" someone called. "Get back here, you little—" The housekeeper appeared, her words cutting off the moment she saw Helena. Hurrying forward, she grabbed hold of the little girl, Mary, and tugged her away from Helena. Mary's face only grew all the more pale. "Beggin' your pardon, miss. We didn't mean to bother any of Lady Andrews's guests."

Helena nodded. For the first time, Helena's eyes dropped away from Mary's pale face and she took in the young girl's dress—old, faded, horribly patched, and drenched.

"What happened?" Helena asked.

The housekeeper seemed unsure about explaining to Helena. But after a moment's pause, she said, "She tipped over the laundry, this one did."

Well, that explained both the crash and the suds clinging to the girl.

"I'm sorry to have bothered you, miss," the housekeeper hurried on. Turning Mary by her shoulders, she pushed her back toward the kitchen. As they walked away, the housekeeper spoke in a hushed, stern tone. "You weren't hired to cause everyone else more work. I've half a mind to throw you and your brother back out into the cold where I found you."

"No, ma'am, please—"

Helena could hear no more as they moved deeper into the manor.

She watched them go, her heart weighed down with worry. Suppose the housekeeper really did throw Mary and her brother out? She'd like to think that the housekeeper was only making threats, only seeing to it that Mary never did something like spill the laundry out again. It was December, after all. Surely the housekeeper wasn't that hard-hearted. But Helena couldn't be sure. She didn't know the woman in the least. Her tone certainly made her sound intent on seeing

Mary gone. And Helena could not forget the undeniable fear on the little girl's face.

Helena picked up her skirt and hurried after the two. "Pardon me," she called out.

The housekeeper stopped with her hand against a door, probably the kitchen door, and waited as Helena caught up.

Helena opened her mouth but hesitated. What could she say to convince this woman that keeping Mary was the sensible thing to do? Helena had no authority at Hedgewood Manor, so it wasn't as though she could simply insist on Mary staying.

"Is there something I can do for you?" the housekeeper asked at length. Her words were proper, but her tone was still heavy and curt.

"Actually, I was thinking"—but not thinking fast enough to come up with something better than a stuttering start—"you should keep the girl on. For now, at least." Apparently thinking up convincing arguments on her feet was not one of Helena's strong suits.

"Oh?" was all the housekeeper said.

Mary looked up at Helena, a sliver of hope etched in her eyes. It was all Helena needed to see.

"Certainly. But more for yourself than anything else," Helena said, an idea finally forming. "After all, I am certain with a house full of guests and all the festivities soon to be upon us, you have much to see after just now." Helena could tell by the look in the housekeeper's eye that she was far too right. "I feel confident that Mary won't make such a mistake again. And having her would be better than having no scullery maid in that position at all."

The housekeeper seemed to be mulling it over. Finally, she drew herself up. "I suppose if she cleans up the mess herself and sets everything to right once more, there would be no need to terminate her and her brother's employ just yet."

Mary's whole frame lifted. "Oh, thank ye, ma'am." She

spoke in a heavy Irish accent. She turned to Helena. "And thank ye, miss!"

The housekeeper shook her head disapprovingly and pushed open the kitchen door. "Get along with you now and see that you leave the misses alone."

Mary curtsied twice, then thrice, then another few times as she stepped through the open door and made her way back into the kitchen. Past the little girl was the biggest, soggiest mess Helena had ever beheld before. Near the hearth, a grand pot rested on its side, mounds of white linen spilling from its mouth along with what must have been many buckets worth of soapy water. Helena was fairly certain that was one of her own undergarments draped atop the rim of the pot.

Mary may still have her position, but she would no doubt be up quite late into the night seeing to this mess.

"Never you fear, miss," the housekeeper said, allowing the door to swing shut, blocking Helena's view of the kitchen, "this shall be taken care of right away. And," she lowered her voice a bit, "I would be grateful if you didn't bandy what you've seen about."

"You can depend on my discretion."

"Thank you, miss. I shall see that the girl is properly reprimanded. This won't happen again."

"Excuse my boldness, but was this the girl's first misstep?"

"Well, yes, I believe so."

"Then I would think that she has been reprimanded enough. No doubt she will see to it that the laundry doesn't tip over again."

The housekeeper drew herself up a bit. "Miss, I don't mean to speak out of turn . . ."

Oh dear, Helena had probably pushed further than she ought. But the way little Mary had looked at her, so afraid of being sent away, she couldn't help herself.

"But this girl and her brother," the housekeeper said,

"came knocking on the kitchen door only two days ago, begging to be hired. I would have turned them away immediately, only, as you have already pointed out, we are sorely stretched seeing to all the needs of Lady Andrews's guests. Not that I'm complaining, mind you."

"Of course." Helena would not blame the housekeeper if she *did* complain a bit. A dozen more people to cook and clean for could not be easy. "Still, I am glad you hired them both. I would hate to think that they were out in the dead of winter with no shelter or food."

The housekeeper went so far as to scoff softly. "There are dozens of children with no shelter or food every winter, miss. It isn't our place to house them all."

Helena's jaw grew tight. Even overworked, how could one woman be so unfeeling? "Certainly Hedgewood Manor cannot take them all in, but those two, at least, have honest work. Of that, I'm glad."

She took hold of her skirt in both hands, ready to leave the corridor in high enough dudgeon to make the housekeeper think twice about speaking so dismissively of those below her. As she marched off, Helena couldn't help but glance back. The housekeeper, with her back to Helena, opened the kitchen door and moved inside.

Mary stood just beside the door; she'd probably been there the whole time listening to the housekeeper and Helena. The girl was watching her, though it wasn't gratitude so much as curiosity which tugged at her features now. Helena shot her a quick smile and left.

It wasn't exactly the sort of interaction she'd imagined having when Emma had first invited her to join the holiday festivities. Nonetheless, it was most satisfying to know she had, in a small way, helped see to it that one little girl and one little boy would not go cold or hungry this season.

CHAPTER NINE

"It is such a warm day," Emma said to the room in general. As a clear response to everyone's surprised expressions, she quickly added, "For December, that is."

Helena would have agreed had she not been so preoccupied. The chessboard between herself and Lord Ellis was demanding all of her attention. She could either move the pawn nearest her knight or her queen. Moving the queen felt risky, but moving the pawn wouldn't garner her much. In a manner, moving the pawn might prove *more risky* than moving the queen.

"Would it be dreadful of me to admit I am tired of being indoors?" one of Lord Chapman's sisters complained. Helena didn't bother turning around to see which one; she wouldn't have been able to tell by looking at them anyway.

"Of course not, dear," Lady Andrews cooed. "It is rather trying for young people to be forever stuck inside."

"Your turn, Miss Spencer." Clearly, Lord Ellis was losing his patience.

"I realize that," she said, struggling to keep her own tone even. Playing chess had always been more fun when she was a child. Picking up her white queen, she slid it across the squares and placed it nearer the black king, but not too close.

"Ha." Lord Ellis tossed his head back and crowed. His dark hair barely moved, however, no doubt due to an inordinate amount of pomade. He moved his knight over a bishop and toppled her white queen over.

Helena pursed her lips and concentrated on the board. Most women she knew would have told her to giggle at her own mistakes and stop trying to win. After all, she could save face by pretending to not even try and then shrug off losing. But Helena hated to feign ignorance. It wasn't likely that she would actually win, but she wasn't going to let that stop her from trying.

She placed her fingers atop the pawn. Perhaps she should have moved it to begin with. Then, at least, she would still have her queen.

A soft cough drew her gaze up, past Lord Ellis, to where Lord Chapman stood beside a bookshelf. He appeared to be reading labels off the shelf. Subtly, he shook his head, his gaze not leaving the books.

Had he been shaking his head *at her*? It felt foolish to assume so, yet, something inside her told her that's exactly what he'd done. She lifted her fingers and slowly moved them across the other pieces, hoping she appeared to be thinking intently on her next move. She was, after all. Just not in the way she hoped Lord Ellis understood her to be.

As her fingers brushed against her remaining knight, Lord Chapman's head moved down and then up in a long nod. His hand came up, his finger flipping upward and to the left before he placed it against a book midway up the shelf.

Helena looked down at the board. She wasn't fully convinced that she *wasn't* imagining Lord Chapman's help. For all she knew, he was engrossed in his own thoughts. Or he *was* suggesting she move her knight, but that didn't necessarily mean he was any kind of an expert at chess. Then again, what did she have to lose? She certainly wasn't going to win *without* his help.

She picked up the knight, moved it forward two, and to the left one, setting it down beside Lord Ellis's rook. He didn't crow over her this time. Next, he moved his king forward. Helena let her hand slip over the pieces, surreptitiously watching Lord Chapman all the while. He nodded in that same, long motion as she reached her rook. He *was* signaling to her. Helena bit back her smile. Perhaps all was not lost after all. Back and forth the game continued. Helena managed to take a pawn. Lord Ellis took her bishop. She took a rook. He took her last knight.

Helena moved her fingers over the few remaining pieces she still had on the board. A pawn, two rooks, a bishop, and, of course, her king. It was possible to win with so few pieces, she knew, but Lord Ellis had far more and it was making maneuvering hard. Lord Chapman's head, instead of nodding as she expected, simply rocked side to side. He seemed as unsure as she was.

There was always the pawn. She'd been wanting to move it for many turns now but hadn't. If she could only move it forward a few squares more, she could get her queen back. But Lord Ellis would see it coming; there was no way to hide such a move. Still, she placed two fingers on the small pawn and pushed it forward. Lord Ellis smiled and Helena knew she'd lost.

Wrapping nearly his whole hand around his bishop he moved it forward, directly over the square her pawn had been on, and halfway across the board.

"Checkmate!" Not giving her so much as a minute to respond, he stood and stalked off, strutting like he'd just defeated Napoleon himself.

"Perfect timing," Emma said, rushing over to Helena. "We

were all just saying how much we would enjoy a turn about the gardens. Care to join us?"

"All right," she muttered, watching Lord Ellis march off, probably to tell the other gentlemen how he'd defeated her so soundly. Well, that was one eligible bachelor she could tell Emma to stop worrying over. Paragon or no, she could not see herself the wife of a man like that.

Emma hurried away, inviting all in the room to change into warmer attire so that they might stroll comfortably out of doors. Helena's gaze moved to Lord Chapman. He caught her eye and gave her a small shrug.

"Sorry," he mouthed, wordlessly.

She waved it off with a hand. It wasn't his fault she'd lost; all he'd tried to do was help. She may not have won, but he had at least helped her make Lord Ellis's win slightly more difficult to come by. And the little bit of subterfuge had been quite diverting. If the whole room had not been present, she may have walked over and told him as much but thought better of it lest she tip her hand to Lord Ellis. She might have lost all interest in pursuing the man, but she'd still rather he not believe her a cheat. Instead, she offered Lord Chapman a simple smile; hopefully, he would understand that she meant it as a thank you.

He smiled back.

Helena's stomach flipped at the sight. She blinked and forced her eyes away. Good heavens, but he was handsome when he smiled. Quite enough to make any woman weak in the knees. It was rather a wonder a man like that hadn't been snatched up already. The thought turned sour. He *had* almost been snatched up. *By her*. Not that it had been her doing at all, but between the late Lord Chapman passing earlier that year and the scandal surrounding the two of them, it was quite logical he had not had the wherewithal to form any attachments. Helena scowled at her own foolishness.

"Hurry up, Helena," Emma said, taking her hand and pulling her upward. "Get your pelisse and fur-lined bonnet ready. We're meeting in the back parlor in a quarter of an hour."

The room was already nearly empty of everyone except Lady Andrews and Lady Shakerley. It seemed Emma was not the only one who was tired of being indoors. Even Lord Chapman was making his way out and into the corridor. So he was going to walk outside with them, too? Helena realized that she hoped he would.

Side by side, she and Emma left the drawing room and headed up the stairs.

Emma leaned in and kept her voice low. "How are things with Lord Ellis? Any interest blooming there?"

"I hope not," Helena whispered back. "I can say most definitively that he is one gentleman you can mark off your list of prospects."

"Oh." Emma pouted. "That only leaves two others. Are you sure you won't reconsider? He very well may improve upon better acquaintance."

"No, thank you. I am quite sure."

Emma was kind enough to not say anything more and they separated as they reached their bedchambers. Helena chose her warmest pelisse, one in velvety blue, and a matching bonnet to go with it. Pulling it on, Helena paused and fingered the soft sleeve. Father had bought this for her only months before he'd unexpectedly passed. Heavens, what would he think of her now if he could see her, vying for the attentions of nearly any and all eligible gentlemen? Would he be disappointed? Would he understand?

She had been robbed of her last remaining bit of family when he'd passed. If he could look down on her from heaven as he always said her mother could do, surely he'd see how lonely she was. How much she wanted a place to belong. Some*one* with whom to belong.

Helena shook away the melancholy. The hurt always struck at the oddest of times. She would be fine for days, sometimes weeks, and then it would rear its painful head once more. But she had other things to occupy herself with just now. She pulled the bedchamber door open and hurried down to the back parlor.

The room was small and with so many people packed inside, quite full. Though she searched most diligently, Helena didn't see Lord Chapman among all the greatcoats and top hats.

Emma slipped up behind her, wearing a maroon pelisse and a cream-colored bonnet. Helena tried, and not for the first time, to tamp down the bit of jealousy that arose at seeing her friend's dark curls against the deep red fabric across her shoulder. Auburn hair was striking, though never fashionable. But the worst part of it was how it limited what one could wear. Maroon was strictly out of the question as far as Helena was concerned.

"Who are you looking for?" Emma asked, "Topper or Lord Forbes?"

Helena opened her mouth, and the truth nearly slipped free. She wasn't looking for either of those gentlemen. She thought better of such a confession at the last minute. "No one, in particular. I was just surprised at how many of Lady Andrews's house guests you were able to convince to join us."

"If I had been born a male, I would surely rule Parliament. That's what my mother is always saying." She slipped her arm around Helena's and her voice dropped softer. "But a word of advice. You *ought* to be looking for someone in particular. A man will never notice a woman who doesn't make him feel noticed first."

"Please tell me you didn't overhear that on-dit from Miss Wynn."

"Oh no, I overheard it from someone equally nasty during the Season." Emma giggled.

Helena was one part appalled, and one larger part diverted. "I sincerely hope you are blessed with many daughters one day. You will make an excellent conniving Mama."

"I know." Emma sighed.

Not two minutes later, it was determined that all who cared to take a turn outside were gathered. The back doors were opened, and they all hurried out as quickly as the cold air rushed in. It was a merry way to spend a bit of the afternoon. The rose bushes were covered in snow, but the paths were easy enough to walk. Helena spoke a bit with Topper and then with Lord Chapman's sisters. Though she sincerely wanted to, Helena didn't ask outright where their brother was. Still, she gathered from their wandering conversation that he'd had to stay behind, at the house, to help their mother with something.

"I have an idea," Miss Wynn called out. "Let us all go wander about the hedge maze. What fun it will be!"

Immediately, everyone agreed.

Everyone except Helena.

As people rushed forward, hurrying down the gentle slope and toward the entrance, Helena's own steps slowed until she was rooted to the ground at the edge of the rose garden path. She was still several paces away. From where she stood, Helena could see over the top of the first few rows. Perhaps it should have made the maze feel less intimidating since she stood above it. Instead, it only started her heart pounding. The dark, weaving path between the hedges appeared to her like a long, black snake—one she had now seen more than once or twice in her nightmares and far too many times to trust. Just looking at the maze made her skin crawl.

"What is it, Helena?" Lady Christina—or perhaps it was

Lady Eleanor—asked. She stood with her twin, Lady Emma, and Topper. The others had all hurried on and were already inside the maze.

This was silly and foolish and ridiculous. A nightmare or two did not mean the giant maze was truly dangerous. Walking between the towering hedges may *feel* unsafe but going in with others, as she was, couldn't truly be dangerous. She closed her eyes for a minute and willed her feet to carry her forward.

It didn't work.

Moreover, her breathing grew rapid and her head tingled with too much air. Good heavens, she felt like she very well might faint.

"Are you all right?" Topper asked.

Helena shook her head and looked back up. "Pardon me, but I think I am getting too cold. I shall just return to the house. You all go ahead without me." Just thinking of returning to the house helped her quick breaths to calm.

The sisters watched her closely, both clearly unsure. Emma, standing back a few paces where no one but Helena would see her expression, was giving Helena an intense don't-you-dare-go-back-inside-now stare.

But she hadn't told Emma about her nightmares; she hadn't told anyone. And she wasn't about to now.

"I can see you back," Topper offered.

Emma's scowl morphed instantly into a bright, this-is-even-better smile.

"No, that is quite all right." She would feel guilty if he missed out on something he'd seemed quite excited about before. Moreover, she didn't feel like justifying herself or making conversation. "I can see the house quite plainly. It is only a short walk back. I shall be fine."

Emma's scowl was back. Helena would have to explain later. For now, all she could do was spin on her heel and hurry back toward the house. As she slipped in through the back parlor, she paused halfway across the room. If she went back into the drawing room, there was a good chance she'd be pulled into a longwinded conversation with Lady Andrews, Lady Shakerley, and possibly Lady Chapman. She liked all three matrons well enough but explaining to those sharp minds why she'd suddenly left the other 'young people' would not be easy.

Instead, she hurried up the stairs before anyone could catch and question her. She still felt a bit shaken from the terror which had unexpectedly gripped her earlier, but being in the warm house was quickly easing the last of her panic. Nonetheless, she didn't feel like hiding out in her bedchamber where she had nothing to do but wonder why the maze had scared her so. Untying the ribbon beneath her chin, Helena pulled her bonnet off. As she did so, her gaze crossed over two closed doors on the other side of the landing.

The library. Perfect. She could easily spend an afternoon in there, with no one asking her questions and without becoming the least bit bored. Not bothering to leave her pelisse and bonnet with her abigail first, Helena turned herself in the direction of the library.

CHAPTER TEN

Fredrick watched his mother closely as she lifted the teacup to her mouth. Was it just a play of the firelight, or was she trembling slightly? She'd complained of a drafty room when they'd first arrived, but he'd spoken to Lord Andrews and that had been fixed immediately. As he'd told Mother, their host and hostess were only too happy to remove her to a different room where she was more comfortable.

She hadn't complained about her new room. Was that because she was comfortable here, or because she worried she would be too much of a burden if she requested a change yet again?

Fredrick lifted his own tea and motioned toward the room around them. "Is this bedchamber more to your liking, Mother?"

"Yes," was her simple reply.

Fredrick wished Father had had more time before he passed to explain to him how to better understand Mother . . . and Christina and Eleanor . . . or any woman for that matter. His mind jumped back to Miss Spencer and the game of chess. At least *she* had understood him. And he, her, if only for a few minutes. Though a lot of good it did her.

"You wanted to go walking outside, didn't you?" Mother said with a sigh.

Fredrick had, but his heart hadn't been set on it. "I am quite content sitting with you."

"No, you're not." She sounded angry. Fredrick sat up. Mother hardly ever got angry. "You're young and you want to be out there with everyone else. You *should* be out there. If you hurry, you can catch up, I am sure of it."

Fredrick wasn't. "Is that what Father would have done? Leave you when you wished for company?"

She scowled at him. "You know he wouldn't have."

Apparently, that had been an unwelcome statement. Heaven help him, he didn't understand why.

Instead, he tried, "They're probably nearly ready to return inside by now. It may be warm for December, as Lady Emma pointed out, but that doesn't mean it's warm enough to stay out long. Don't worry about me. If I had wanted to go outside walking, I would have."

"Nonsense." She slammed her teacup and saucer back onto the low table between them. "You should go."

"I'm serious, Mother. It's too late—"

"Go." She lifted a single eyebrow as though challenging him to defy her.

His father may have never explained the intricate workings of female expressions, but one thing he had made exceedingly clear was that Fredrick was never to defy his mother.

Fredrick shook his head and slowly stood. "If that's what you wish, I will leave." Perhaps she just needed some peace and quiet. A few minutes to herself. It was the only logical reason he could come up with for her sudden dismissal. She'd all but bodily tossed him from the room. He thought she'd been enjoying his presence. Apparently not.

He moved down the corridor. He didn't care to try and join the group outside now. He was sure he'd only show up in time for everyone else to declare themselves too cold and intent on returning. His steps slowed as he reached the landing. With everyone else outside, he wasn't sure what to do with himself.

Placing hands on hips, he turned slightly. He could always return to his bedchamber, but nothing more interesting than well-painted walls awaited him there. He slowly turned back, his gaze crossing over an open library door.

Or, he could get a new book. Lord Andrews had assured him he was welcome to any books inside, and he had finished *Tom Jones* two days prior. Perhaps if he ventured to read that book his sisters were always speaking of, he'd understand them better. What was it called? *Sense and Sensibility*, that's what it was. It wouldn't hurt to read a few passages at the very least. He strode forward and through the open door. The smell of old books rushed to greet him.

The wall directly to Fredrick's left was covered floor to ceiling in books, as was the wall in front of him, save the very center which was reserved for windows. The center of the room was full of furniture. Chairs by the fire, a settee beneath the window—all things that were comfortable and well-suited to reading. This had been a good choice. He strode into the room; something small resting against the nearest chair caught his eye. It appeared to be a dark blue ribbon.

He stepped around the chair and found a bonnet discarded upon the seat, a matching pelisse resting beside it. The floor creaked along the other side of the room. He wove between chairs and tables toward the far wall. Like the left side of the room, the right wall was floor to ceiling books. Only, he couldn't see who, or what, had made the sound.

Finally, he stepped around a large wingback and discovered Miss Spencer, kneeling on the floor, pulling book after book off the shelf. She already had nearly half a dozen tucked up close to her, balanced by one arm. She added first one and then another as he watched.

"Seems we had the same idea," he said.

Miss Spencer jumped, a squeak escaping from her. The book tower in her arms tumbled all around, books smacking against the floor and flopping open. Miss Spencer reared back, lost her balance, and landed hard on her seat.

Fredrick hurried forward. "I am so sorry. I had no intention of startling you." He reached out a hand and she slipped hers into it. The same heat he'd felt when she'd placed her hand on his arm several days ago returned. Though they both wore gloves, he could feel the pressure of her palm, and it sent his skin tingling.

The moment she was standing and had righted herself, he pulled his hand away. What was happening? Whatever it was, it had to stop. Nothing could ever happen between them; he'd nearly ruined her life as it was.

Miss Spencer was busy brushing herself off and shaking out her skirt, allowing Fredrick a moment to compose himself. Several curls hung loosely about her face and down the back of her neck, probably pulled loose when she'd removed her bonnet. She stood straight once more, and their eyes met. He'd always been rather partial toward green eyes.

"Please accept my apology," Lord Chapman said with a proper bow.

Helena was more than willing to forgive him; if only her heart would calm down long enough for her to collect herself and speak coherently. He'd startled her soundly.

"Poor form, Lord Chapman," she teased. "First you make me lose at chess, and now you nearly give me a heart attack." She tsked softly, even as her heartbeat finally eased.

"You're right. I guess I have a couple of things to apologize for." He smiled, that same slight tip of the lips that had made her stomach flip earlier. Bending down, he gathered up the spilled books.

Helena shook herself then knelt down to help.

"You know," she said, "I used to believe I was quite proficient at chess. But then I started playing people who were not my father, and I quickly learned otherwise."

He chuckled. "I used to feel the same way about being a gentleman." With the books shared between them, they stood.

"What do you mean by that?" she asked.

His smile turned a bit sad. The sight pulled on Helena's heart. "I used to believe I was quite good at it, and then my father passed. Now that I'm the Earl of Chapman, I feel far less competent."

Helena placed her stack of books down on a small table, situated between two large wingbacks with lion-paw feet. She spoke of her father often enough with Emma, but her friend could never fully understand. "It's a hole in one's chest, is it not?" Helena sat down in one of the chairs.

Lord Chapman placed his books on the table beside hers. "I'm beginning to wonder if it ever goes away." His voice was as heavy as she felt.

"Maybe it will someday. But if it does, I haven't reached that point yet."

"That's not very reassuring," he said, sitting in the matching wingback and giving her a melancholy smile.

"No, I suppose not."

They held one another's gazes for a moment. It was a sad sort of conversation, yet one she was so very happy to finally have with someone who understood.

Lord Chapman tipped his head to the side and looked away. "There are so many things I wish I could ask him."

Helena nodded. She could relate to that.

"Like how to see to multiple estates at once," Lord Chapman spoke on.

"How to know if there is a way to invest a small sum of money, and turn it into enough to secure one's future," Helena added.

"Or how to handle dissent in Parliament."

"How to handle saying goodbye to a houseful of servants, pack up one's life, and move in with a friend."

"How to care for an aging mother, or how to properly guide one's sisters."

"How to plan a funeral." The room began to blur around her. Helena blinked several times, and hot tears rolled down her cheeks.

A hand wrapped around hers. "I should not have spoken on so."

"Are you apologizing again, Lord Chapman?"

His chuckle was far more dry this time. "It seems to be the only thing I ever do where you are concerned." He pressed a handkerchief into her hand.

She took it and dabbed at her eyes. "I keep thinking that one of these days, I'll hear his name, or he'll be brought up in conversation and I *won't* be reduced to a watering pot."

"Someday you will. But if today isn't that day, that's all right, too."

Helena felt the tightness in her chest ease. Gracious, but it was so nice to speak with someone who understood. Someone who didn't grow uncomfortable at her blatant show of emotion. Father had always been that person for her. As she now knew that she wasn't actually good at chess, she also now knew that having a father who was both a financial support and an emotional support was not common. She only wished she'd appreciated him more when he'd been alive.

"I swear most days I get through without a problem," she

said, "and then, it'll hit me again, wholly unexpectedly, and every bit as overwhelming as if he'd passed yesterday."

"Ah, blast," Lord Chapman said, dropping his head into his upturned hands.

Helena looked up at him in surprise.

He shook his head with a groan. "Of course. That's why she threw me out."

"Don't tell me I'm not the only lady you find yourself in need of apologizing to."

He ran both hands through his hair. "It's my mother," he said, lifting his head once more. Helena tried to suppress her foolish grin. He did look ever so alluring with his hair tousled and his sincere eyes focused on her.

"Not two hours ago," he continued, "I forwent walking outside because she seemed lonely and out of sorts. I sat with her in her room, and I ordered us up some tea. I thought we were having a splendid time. Then, quite suddenly, she grew upset and demanded I leave." He pushed against his knees and leaned heavily back against the chair. "That's why I came in here in the first place."

"You believe she's missing your father?"

"It makes sense now that I think of it. She often grew out of sorts at the littlest things those first couple of months. She's been better as of late, so I hadn't even thought . . ." He sighed and shrugged.

"What used to help her?"

"Time alone. Or, at least, that's what I gave her." He threw his hands up. "I don't know. Maybe that's not at all what she needed. But it always worked eventually, so I kept doing it." He laughed derisively. "Some son I turned out to be."

"I'm sure you're doing a far better job than you think."

"That would be nice to believe." His gaze held hers. It was as though everything else—the room full of books, the house full of guests—all faded away. There was him, there was her.

An easy conversation where she didn't have to pretend or hide, where she didn't have to worry about how he thought of her or what rumors might be circulating. His disheveled curls falling over his forehead. His hopeful smile and the way it warmed her heart.

Lord Chapman cleared his throat and twisted about in his chair, facing her more directly. "I feel I ought to avail myself of this opportunity and apologize for something else."

The closeness which had enveloped them seemed to morph from comfortable to agitated. Helena had a good guess where this was headed.

"I find it strange," he said, "that our lives have impacted one another's so dramatically, yet this is the first time we've ever truly spoken."

"It is a bit backward, is it not?"

"Indeed. Let me say now that I am deeply regretful for the happenings earlier this year. I sincerely apologize for the part I played."

Helena turned and faced him as well. "May I be bold? It was never made clear to me exactly *what part* you did play. I know Lord Shakerley met with you, or perhaps a relation of yours? The details were never explained."

"Ah, well, that explains the pepper in my coffee."

Helena couldn't stop the small laugh that escaped. He gave her an answering smile. It was so nice to be able to laugh and smile, even during what, with anyone else, would have been a very heavy conversation.

"Perhaps after I hear your side of the tale," she said, "I may need to apologize as well."

"No. I still deserved it. The truth is this: my uncle, Mr. Baker, is the one who first spoke with Lord Shakerley. They formed the design all on their own. It was only after the contract had been written up that Baker spoke to me of it. I immediately rebuffed all talk of marriage contracts and demanded he end things with Lord Shakerley. At the time, my cousin, Alice, assured me that no one besides the few of us involved in the contract knew of the possible engagement and that nothing would ever come of it."

It did help to know where he stood. She and Lord Shakerley got along well enough, but there was no close connection there, and she hadn't felt comfortable pressing him for details. "Thank you for telling me."

He reached out, placing a hand against her arm. "If helping you find a husband this Christmas is what you want, then I will gladly do so as my penance."

It was too bad they were only just now getting to know one another. She could have used such a sincere friend these past several months. Emma was wonderful, but sometimes she got ideas in her head and forgot to listen to anything anyone else had to say.

"It isn't so much what I want as it is a necessity at this point. But, it's one I've resigned myself to. And I am having a jolly time getting to know new people." But enough of that. "However, there is a question I've been meaning to ask you."

Lord Chapman leaned back, his demeanor calm and relaxed. "Ask away."

"How *do* you tell Lady Christina and Lady Eleanor apart?"

CHAPTER ELEVEN

Helena sat atop Emma's bed. It was a shame she couldn't lie down. But her abigail had already finished her up-do for the evening and resting back against the soft coverlet and obliging pillow would only ruin her hair.

"I think Topper is growing quite fond of you," Emma said from her seat in front of the mirror. Her abigail had been forced to redo Emma's hair when Lady Shakerley had stepped in moments before and declared the style far too similar to last Season's.

"Do you?" Helena answered, pulling her thoughts away from the soft bed beneath her. "He's polite and attentive, but I don't sense any partiality on his part."

"He's *polite* and *attentive*; what more do you expect?"

Helena shook her head. It was just a feeling, something in her stomach. "I think you are reading too much into it. I've seen him be polite and attentive toward every woman here."

Emma let out an unladylike grunt and waved a hand over her shoulder at Helena. "You are being too particular."

No, Emma didn't understand. Helena was in no way expecting, or even wishing, to end the house party with an ardent declaration of love from any gentleman. However, didn't a man show at least *some* partiality toward a woman he meant to pursue? Even when it was only with the idea of making a mutually beneficial match? Topper *had* been a fine partner at cards and the like, but she just couldn't see him offering for her.

Perhaps she should have asked Lord Chapman yesterday afternoon when they had spoken in the library. He was the closest thing she had to a brother—closest thing she'd *ever* had to a brother.

Then again, the term 'brother' didn't seem quite right. She somehow couldn't see her stomach responding the way it did to Lord Chapman's smile if he were her sibling.

"What of Lord Ellis, then?" Emma pressed.

"Oh, please, no." One chess game had been enough to solidify her opinion of him.

"Beggars should be no choosers," Emma intoned.

Helena was sorely tempted to finish the familiar phrase, "but yet they will". She thought better of it. Based on the look her friend was giving her, Helena was fairly sure they were both thinking it anyway.

"Then," Emma said, scowling at Helena through the mirror, "we shall have to focus our efforts on Lord Forbes. You could certainly do worse than being connected to his well-known deep pockets."

Lord Forbes's wealth was certainly often spoken of, and he was pleasing enough to look at, though Helena preferred Lord Chapman's features. More still, she liked the way Lord Chapman had taken her hand when she was mourning her father anew, and how expressive his face became when he spoke about his sisters.

"I like that smile," Emma said, standing. Her abigail must have finally finished. "I think Lord Forbes might be just the man for you."

Helena wasn't about to tell Emma that she'd been thinking of Lord Chapman and not Lord Forbes at all. Besides, whatever smile had been on her face was there because she was remembering the stories Lord Chapman had shared all about how Lady Christina and Lady Eleanor had pretended to be one another on ever so many occasions. It had nothing to do with a growing tendre for anyone in particular.

Even if she ever *were* to meet a man who drew her to him, how would it end? Though she and Emma hadn't spoken of it, not a day at Hedgewood Manor had passed without Helena happening upon one conversation or another regarding herself. Sometimes they were mostly innocent, as when she'd entered the back drawing room and overheard Lady Andrews.

"Just to look at her, I'm not surprised so many people wondered if she *wasn't* cast aside because of some indiscretion, as beautiful as she is. That was, of course, before I knew her better."

Other comments were less accommodating, such as Miss Wynn's almost-whisper. "Have you seen the way Lord Ellis looks at her? I can't tell if he's dreaming up something awful and unseemly, or *remembering*."

Emma placed her hand on Helena's arm, ending the long train of disheartening memories. Emma looked at her with her brow creased. Helena shook her head and reassured her friend with a smile, but Emma seemed unwilling to believe that she was all right. Truly, the last thing Helena wanted was to have it out and explain all she'd heard these past few weeks. It wasn't as though any of it was new. Before Emma could press her, Helena brought up a new subject.

"Emma," Helena said, standing and moving closer to her friend. "If I wanted to see a man of business, to consult me on the small bit of money my father left me, do you believe your father would accompany me?" Uncle Scrooge had not responded to her letter. But she remembered, while speaking with Lord Chapman, that her father had once said that Scrooge was a well-respected investor. Since she didn't want to admit to the Shakerleys just yet that she did, in fact, have a living relative, even one who refused to acknowledge any relation, this seemed a good excuse to go and meet the man in person. Of course, her father had also mentioned that Uncle Scrooge's profession was what had caused the rift between him and Mother. But, perhaps it could also serve as the means Helena needed to see him in person.

Emma's lips tugged to one side. "Didn't he already offer to let you speak with *his* man of business? You won't want to go to a stranger. Suppose this man cheats you out of everything? A woman cannot be too careful where her finances are concerned." Though she didn't say it aloud, Helena got the impression Emma meant "a woman cannot be too careful *especially* when her finances are so paltry."

"But my father recommended this man, in particular." It was a stretch of the truth. Still, she felt confident that Father would want her to seek out her last remaining family relative. Hopefully, her small lie wasn't too much of a sin. "He is located in Dunwell, and we'll likely never be so close again."

"Who would your father possibly have known in Dunwell? I thought most of his business was conducted in London."

Helena's excuse was unraveling fast. "This man wasn't *his* man of business. Only a man he'd heard of and heard good things about."

"It all sounds rather uncertain." Emma looped her arm through Helena's and began pulling her toward the bedchamber door. "It won't signify, either way. You will be married soon, and your finances will be handled by your new husband."

Helena tried to keep her shoulders back as they made their way down the corridor. She could just tell Emma who this man of business was and of his relation to her. But she didn't feel she could just now. It would awaken too many questions: why hadn't the Shakerleys ever met or even heard of Uncle Scrooge before? If Helena's grandfather had disowned his own son, why reach out to him at all? What proof did Helena have her Uncle wasn't a scoundrel or worse?

She very well couldn't go seek him out on her own, so that only left her one option. The same one she'd already tried that had come up short. She would have to write him another letter. Who knew? perhaps if she wrote enough times, he'd finally respond.

Helena hoped he would. But she didn't have much faith.

CHAPTER TWELVE

Fredrick strode down the stairs, tugging his gloves on tightly. He was rather looking forward to horseback riding today. Tomorrow, he would have been at Hedgewood Manor for two weeks, yet this was the first time in all that while that he'd had a chance to get out and ride.

The plans had begun as something he, Topper, Lord Forbes, and Lord Ellis were all intent on doing together. But when Lady Emma had heard of the outing, she'd immediately rallied all the other young ladies and declared they, too, wished to ride. It was probably another attempt at pushing Miss Spencer toward either Topper or Lord Ellis. Or Lord Forbes? He had a hard time keeping up with all the machinations, but he was fairly certain Miss Spencer would never consider Lord Ellis after he had behaved so uncivilly during their chess game.

He neared the bottom of the stairs just in time to catch sight of Miss Spencer hurrying to catch up with the house butler.

"Sorry, miss," the butler responded before she even had a chance to say anything. "No letters today."

Her shoulders fell. With a grim nod, she turned and began to walk off.

Fredrick reached her in only a few strides. "Were you expecting a correspondence?"

"No, but I was hoping all the same."

He offered her his arm and she rested her hand atop it. The heat he'd felt before came again, but he expected it this time—and ignored it. Certainly, he *should* ignore it.

"Truth is, I wrote to my uncle."

Fredrick pulled to an abrupt stop. "Wait—you have an *uncle*?"

She shushed him, glancing about the corridor, but it was empty, save them.

Still, Fredrick obliged and lowered his voice. "I was told in no uncertain terms that you had no near relations left."

She, too, spoke softly. "Mr. Scrooge is my mother's brother. Grandfather disowned him some years ago, a little after my mother passed. Apparently, my uncle and his father had a long and troublesome history. My mother helped ease things between them, or so I was led to believe. But after she was gone, things fell apart rather quickly. He's had no connection with my family for as long as I can remember. He didn't come to Grandfather's funeral. He certainly was not present when my father passed."

"But now you're wanting to mend things?" With no other family left, he could certainly see the pull.

"As of right now, I just want to *hear* from him. I don't believe him to be dead, but he might as well be for all the letters I've received back."

That had to hurt—to know your own uncle didn't even care enough to write back even though he was your last remaining relative. That was a loneliness Fredrick could only imagine. He, at least, still had Mother and Christina and Eleanor and plenty of uncles and aunts and cousins besides.

Miss Spencer pressed her hand more firmly atop his arm. "Please don't mention this to the Shakerleys. They know nothing of my uncle, not that he exists nor that I've written him."

He covered her hand with one of his own. "If that is your wish." It felt strangely good to have her beside him. More still, once they entered the drawing room and she left his side to speak with his sisters, he felt her absence every bit as acutely.

He wasn't left long to dwell on the fact that he remained aware of Miss Spencer as she moved about the room, for Lady Emma bore down on him like a fox chasing a rabbit.

"We have a problem," she said, with no preamble. "Today's ride was supposed to be a chance for Helena to spend time with Lord Forbes."

Lady Emma's declaration brought a new emotion, one that Fredrick refused to analyze or label. "I happen to know Lord Forbes is quite looking forward to today's ride."

"Yes, but so are your sisters and Miss Wynn. Now, Lord Forbes, I have learned, enjoys more of a rousing ride. Helena is an excellent horsewoman and will keep up without hesitation, I am confident."

Fredrick wasn't surprised to learn Miss Spencer was excellent on a horse. It seemed to fit her fiery hair, not to mention her readiness to control her own future by reaching out to an estranged family member.

"Neither Christina nor Eleanor will want more than a casual trot, so you needn't worry where they are concerned. Besides, you could just tell them Miss Spencer wishes to speak with Lord Forbes."

Lady Emma shook her head and pursed her lips at what she clearly deemed an insensible suggestion. "I'm not worried about them. Even now they are busy speaking with Topper. The real problem is Miss Wynn. Do you know if she is a good horsewoman?"

"I have never seen her ride, but I believe she is."

Lady Emma pulled a face. "She is monopolizing him even now."

Fredrick followed Lady Emma's gaze. True enough, Miss Wynn was speaking quite animatedly to Lord Forbes and seemed unlikely to let him go any time soon.

"You need to take care of her," Lady Emma said.

"Pardon me?"

"Strike up a conversation. Distract her away from Lord Forbes. Flirt with her."

A lump inside Fredrick's throat was steadily growing with each of Lady Emma's suggestions. "I feel now might be a good time to point out that I don't flirt with women I'm not interested in. I'm no cad."

"Pretend you're one just for the afternoon. You owe Helena that much, at the very least."

His gaze jumped to Miss Spencer; she was laughing at something Christina had said. She looked lovely in her dark brown riding habit. The dark tone set off her hair in a most flattering way.

"Very well." He sighed. "I'll see what I can do."

This was *not* going to be the pleasant afternoon on horseback he'd been looking forward to. He strode over to Miss Wynn.

"Good afternoon," he said. Miss Wynn turned toward him, a bit of surprise showing in her eyes. Lord Forbes looked relieved. Fredrick wished he could somehow secretly communicate with the man. If he could, he'd say, "Run, while you have the chance." Judging by Lord Forbes's understated, yet understandable, expression, he'd take it, too.

Fredrick turned toward Miss Wynn. "That is a very beautiful riding habit."

She twisted back and forth, sending her skirt twirling

slightly. "Why thank you, Lord Chapman. How kind of you to notice."

The way she simpered and fluttered her lashes made him slightly sick. Fredrick shot Miss Spencer a glance, but she wasn't looking his way and so didn't see. If he could secretly communicate with *her*, he would have said, "This is for you. Trust me when I say, I'm not doing it for myself."

CHAPTER THIRTEEN

"Such fine horses." Eleanor giggled as she stroked one down its long nose.

"Yes, they are," Helena agreed. It was only the two of them in the stable, everyone else having already made their way back to the house. Their not-so-small outing had been enjoyable, though not for the reasons Emma had hoped.

Oh, Lord Chapman had been a sport and kept Miss Wynn occupied the entire time. Furthermore, Emma, Christina, and Eleanor had all carefully, yet purposefully, allowed Helena time to speak with each of the other three gentlemen. At one point, when Christina found herself the center of much attention, she'd gone so far as to fake exhaustion and excuse herself early. Though, Topper had gone with her to see her safely back to the house. It had left them a party of three ladies and only two gentlemen—not counting Lord Chapman or Miss Wynn, as they stayed a little apart and near the back—yet Helena had not had one moment alone.

Her old friend and her two new friends were certainly rallying about her and seeing to it that she had every opportunity to make a match.

Nonetheless, none of that was what had made the evening ride so enjoyable.

No, best of all had been the feel of fresh air against her cheeks, seeing the clear blue sky stretching out over her head, and the feel of the warm beast beneath her, bearing her up. She'd always adored horseback riding but had had so little time for it these past few years. It had been most enjoyable to ride once more. She'd also enjoyed catching bits of conversation from behind her. Apparently, Lord Chapman had truly tried to be a good conversationalist with Miss Wynn, but she hardly let him get a word in edgewise and insisted he agree with her the few times he tried stating his own opinion.

Helena had tried hard not to laugh at his clearly uncomfortable predicament. It was terribly uncharitable of her to do so, especially since he was only in that spot in an effort to help her.

"Did you ride much growing up?" Eleanor asked.

"Oh, yes. All summer long. Especially those years when my father traveled to London on business," she added with a smile. "My favorite mount was a light brown gelding named Butterscotch." How she'd loved that horse.

Eleanor's hand, still stroking a horse's nose, slowed. "I've always had a secret desire to marry a man with ever so many horses."

"You ride exceptionally well," Helena said. It was yet one more small difference between the twins. She would have to tell Lord Chapman; she felt she was finally getting the hang of telling the two apart.

"Thank you." Eleanor's smile was far more shy than any Helena had ever seen the young woman give.

"I am in earnest. You are excellent on horseback. I think you *should* keep your eyes open for a man with many horses. Maybe even a gentleman who runs a stud farm?"

"Oh, no," Eleanor said in a rush. "I don't know about that. I am certain mama expects both Christina and me to marry titled gentlemen."

"So long as he can provide comfortably for you and you are happy, then I am certain she can have nothing against such a match."

"Do you really think so?"

"Yes, I sincerely do." Though Helena hadn't had many conversations with Lady Chapman, she was getting to know her three children quite well. Certainly they would not be the kind, considerate individuals they all were without an equally warmhearted mother.

Helena's heart hurt with a small tinge of regret and longing. She herself had grown up without a mother at all, warmhearted or otherwise. What would her own mother say if she could see the woman Helena had become? Would she be pleased with her attempts to secure a safe future? Would she be upset she hadn't managed to do so before now?

Eleanor's arms wrapped around Helena, drawing her back into the present.

"I'm so glad we're friends," Eleanor said.

Helena returned the hug. "As am I."

Eleanor drew back, but her smile remained. "I think I'm going to lie down for a bit before dinner. Being out too long in the cold always makes me so tired."

Helena could relate. There was something about being outside in winter that could undoubtedly drain a person of their strength. "You go ahead. I think I'll stay here for a bit longer."

Eleanor said she understood and hurried off, leaving Helena to the silence and the horses.

Did she truly understand? Helena watched her friend go. She barely understood herself. Helena was tired, like Eleanor, but more from the strain of always having to smile and be pleasing than from their ride. Since when had being upbeat become a strain? Helena had always prided herself on her optimistic outlook on life. But things had changed when her father passed. Now the constant need to appear cheerful was as much a drain on her strength as the bitterest of cold winds.

How she wished for a place, a moment to simply sit down, cry, and release the weight she was forever carrying.

The time in the library with Lord Chapman came to mind. Truth was, except for Emma, Helena had not allowed herself to cry in front of anyone, not even during her father's funeral. That time with Lord Chapman had been nice. Too bad there was a very good chance it would never happen again.

Stepping carefully to avoid soiling her boots, Helena made her way toward the door. Just as she reached the last stall, the horse inside stretched its nose out toward her.

"Well, good afternoon to you, too," she said. She paused. He was the exact same color Butterscotch had been. Her heart ached anew. Reaching out, she petted the horse down his nose. "Perhaps you and I should take a ride together sometime."

The horse flipped his main and snorted.

Helena laughed. "Lively, aren't you. What's your name? I'll bet it's something blithe."

"His name is Starfire."

The unexpected voice made Helena whirl around. Lord Ellis stood, shoulder leaning against one of the posts between the stalls. His dark greatcoat was almost exactly the same color as his jacket. So much so that, though the greatcoat was open, she could hardly tell where one ended and the other began.

"Did you forget something?" Helena asked, glancing about her. She'd seen him return to the house with everyone else. Still, what would he have left behind that he couldn't have sent a manservant back for?

He stood and walked directly up to her, closer than he'd ever stood before. Helena leaned back slightly at his nearness.

"Oh, I wouldn't say *forgot*, precisely." He was smiling, but it wasn't friendly.

Tingles of warning pricked against her skin. Helena took a step back. "I'm not sure what you mean, sir."

"Well, when I saw that twin return without you and realized you were here alone . . ." He reached out, taking hold of her elbow firmly, and pulled her toward him. "I must say, with all the talk I've heard about you, it does make a man curious." He leaned down, bringing his face closer to her.

Helena pushed away, stumbling out of his grasp. Frantic, she looked about. What could she use if he pursued her? There was no chance she could scream and be heard by anyone in the house, and no stablehands were nearby.

Lord Ellis only laughed. "I was afraid of that." Though his lips were still turned up, his eyes were dark and his expression haughty. "London rumors can prove disappointingly inaccurate." With a shrug, he sauntered toward the door.

He appeared to be leaving—oh, please let him be leaving. Helena's gaze stayed anchored on his as he paused before moving outside.

"However," he said, his back toward her, "should you find yourself in need of entertainment beyond that provided by a simple Christmas house party, know that I, for one, am willing to explore other options with you."

Helena shuddered as he moved out of sight. She reached for a stable door, leaning her full weight against it. She felt hot and then almost immediately cold all over.

Her situation in London had turned most distressing by the time the season had ended but never had such a thing as this happened to her. She'd been so hopeful Hedgewood Manor would help her move *past* the scandal of last summer, not dredge it up in even worse ways.

Helena pulled herself upright. She needed to get back to the house. She couldn't stand staying out here alone any longer.

Alone.

Like she so frequently was. Like she *always* was.

Her legs felt unsteady, but she made her way back to the house, regardless. Blessedly, she didn't see Lord Ellis. How would she face him tonight at dinner? Helena moved inside the house, shut the door, and leaned back against it. She couldn't think about that right now.

All she wanted was to *not* be alone.

Why had she stayed behind in the stable when Eleanor left? She should have simply returned with her friend, then Lord Ellis would not have . . .

She shuddered once more. At least he hadn't actually forced himself upon her. The moment she'd pushed away, he'd released her and left. Helena made her way out to the corridor, glancing about as she walked. Where was Emma? Or Eleanor?

She heard female voices around the corner and hurried that way. But instead of Emma or Eleanor or Christina, it was Lady Shakerley and Lady Chapman. They walked slowly down the wide corridor, looking at the many portraits lining the wall.

Helena approached and, as both women turned her way, pulled on a smile.

"Oh, Helena, dear," Lady Chapman said. "How was your ride?"

She didn't dare speak for fear that her trembling would become obvious, so she only nodded.

"Are you all right?" Lady Shakerley asked.

The question brought tears to her eyes. Helena glanced down, willing her nerves to calm.

An arm stretched around her shoulders and Lady Shakerley pulled her in. "It's been a rather long Christmas so far, hasn't it?"

Lady Shakerley didn't know the half of it. Still, she didn't feel like explaining, and so she simply nodded again.

"Society can be rather unkind," Lady Chapman said.

"And the men rather trying of one's patience," Lady Shakerley added.

"Yet, worth it, when the right one comes along." Lady Chapman's words had a bit of sorrow in them.

Helena pulled back, standing up straight once more. "Thank you. I think I just needed a parent for a few minutes again."

Both women gave her such melancholy smiles; perhaps she shouldn't have said anything.

Lady Shakerley's voice was slow when she next spoke. "You do realize that your problems won't truly go away until you are wed, correct?"

Helena nodded.

"Well," Lady Shakerley continued, her words still slow, "if ever you grow tired of the games and the waiting, I am sure my husband and I can find you someone." She lifted a hand before Helena could object and hurried on. "Someone kind and well off. Someone who would remove all disgrace from your name and allow you to reenter society without worry. And this time, I promise I'll be involved enough that no arrangement would be made without the knowledge and consent of *both* parties."

Helena wanted to be upset. But looking at Lady Shakerley, she knew the woman's offer came from a place of love and concern.

"My marriage with my late husband was arranged," Lady Chapman said, "and we grew to love each other dearly. I thank the Lord every day that my parents were wise enough to put us together."

Perhaps Helena had been rash to assume such was a bad idea. Of course, in terms of being engaged to Lord Chapman, she hadn't had the opportunity to consider it a good idea or not. And she certainly hadn't been consulted when he cried off and left her reputation in tatters.

Now, though, things were different. She *was* being consulted. She *was* going to step up and make sure her future was one where she was safe and protected.

Lady Chapman gave Lady Shakerley a quick sideways glance and then looked back at Helena. "If you are at all interested, I do happen to know a gentleman who would suit quite well."

Her son's face came to Helena's mind.

"I don't know why I didn't think to ask him to join us before," she said.

Then she *wasn't* talking of Lord Chapman. Helena tried not to feel disappointed.

But why would she be? Her and Lord Chapman making a match was a door that had already closed. Most emphatically.

"Do you wish for me to write to him?" Lady Chapman asked.

Gracious, she wanted an answer now? Helena was still reeling from her encounter with Lord Ellis. Could she even handle another gentleman? Another introduction tinged with awkwardness the moment he realized who she was? Another painful period of trying to convince him that all the scandal was fake? Another round of moments wondering what yet another person thought of her?

"I see we have overwhelmed you," Lady Shakerley said. "How about this? We'll have Lady Chapman write the gentleman and *invite* him to join us, but no more. You can get to know him before any more is said on the subject."

She ought to say yes. Another eligible bachelor. Nothing could be more needed. Moreover, both ladies agreed they wouldn't do more than simply have him come and stay for a bit. If she discovered he would never suit, that would be the end of it, and neither party would be embarrassed or worse off.

"All right," Helena said after a bit of their convincing. "Write to him. But I make no promises."

CHAPTER FOURTEEN

The next day, when everyone else chose to take a turn about the gardens, Helena agreed to join. Time outdoors was a precious commodity in the bleakest months of winter. Still, as they walked, Helena found herself lagging further and further behind.

If she could not see Lord Ellis speaking animatedly with Lady Wynn, she would have been wary of distancing herself from the rest of the group. As it was, a little bit of quiet was proving soothing to her soul. She still didn't know how she felt about Lady Chapman writing some gentleman and inviting him—she sincerely hoped Lady Andrews wouldn't be put out by the extra addition.

Helena's gaze moved out past the group of people in front of her—the people who spoke well enough of her when she was around but whispered most unkindly when she wasn't—and focused instead on the tops of the trees in the distant forest. They were a mixture of brown and green, some barren and looking for all to see as though they'd died. Some were still a deep green, their slender pine needles vibrant against the muted colors that surrounded them.

"Watch out," a young voice called out.

Helena glanced about, seeing the large tree root jutting out of the ground barely in time to avoid tripping over it.

With a bit of a skip, she managed to stay on her feet. Helena righted herself and glanced about. She could see no one but could not deny that she'd heard a child call to her.

A second, equally young voice hushed the first.

Helena slowly turned toward the sound. If she wasn't mistaken, the voices had come from off the path to her left. She moved up toward the large tree with the roots that had nearly brought her to her knees and peered around it.

Huddled atop the snow, crouched low with their heads down in their hands, were two small children. They were clearly trying to make themselves as small and hard to see as possible.

"Hello," Helena said.

Both children jumped, their gazes meeting hers. Helena recognized the scullery maid, Mary, at once. The boy at her side was her brother, most likely; his eyes were nearly identical to his sister's.

"Evening, miss," Mary said, scrambling to stand, though one foot immediately dropped several inches into the snow. Once she was standing, moreover, she dropped into a curtsy.

The boy followed suit, bowing beside his sister. He was dressed in the most worn-out pair of breeches Helena had ever seen. Holes tattered the bottom hem while a variety of different colored threads patched up what must have been yet more holes along either leg. Were these two truly in Lord Andrews's employ? Surely someone could have given them something better to wear.

"Shouldn't you be in the kitchen?" Helena directed her question to the girl but kept her voice soft. Both children looked like they may bolt at any minute.

"Yes, miss. Sorry, miss." More curtsying. Then she turned

to her brother and whispered, "Remember, obey the groom like you would Mr. Chant. And no more hiding."

The girl came out from behind the tree, but her brother reached out, stopping her.

"Will he hurt me, too?" the boy asked in a feeble voice.

Helena's heart ached at the sound. The poor thing. And who was this Mr. Chant? An ardent desire to protect these two children rushed through Helena.

"Yes he will," the girl replied without hesitation. "So mind your respecting and hop to."

The boy nodded and pulled out a pitchfork that had been tucked beneath a shrub. It looked far too big for the small lad to be handling all on his own. Walking most awkwardly, he made his way toward the stables.

The girl remained beside Helena. "Please forgive m' brother. He's not as familiar with workin' in a big house as I am."

"I am sure he will learn quickly." Helena hoped it sounded like reassurance. Truly, she wanted so badly to reach out and pull both children into a hug.

"And thank ye," the girl continued, "for speaking to the housekeeper for me. I know she would have done more iffin you hadn't said somethin' to her."

"You are quite welcome. Perhaps we could walk back toward the house together." Helena was growing cold anyway and, though she knew it was quite unheard of for a woman in her station to walk with a scullery maid, she was loath to leave the little girl just yet. Both children seemed quite alone in the world, and so young, too.

"If you wish it, miss."

With the young girl following close beside her, Helena led the way past the stables, the sound of the boy's pitchfork knocking against a wall occasionally echoing behind them.

"Are you enjoying working here at Hedgewood Manor?" Helena asked.

"Oh yes, miss," the girl said. "It is nice to be sleeping indoors again."

Helena's stomach flipped at the thought of both children, huddled together, out in the winter snow all night.

"Yes," she said, "I am sure it is."

"M' brother will make a fine stable boy. I promise. He just don't know all he needs to yet."

"At least he has you. I am sure you will be able to help him understand what is expected of him."

"I try. We may be poor as church mice and in want of much, but at least I knows how a house is runned."

Helena's mind once more turned to her father. He, too, had begun poor. Though the son of a titled gentleman, when he and her mother had married, they hadn't had much. But his knowledge of business and crop rotation had not only saved them but had provided an extremely comfortable life.

"Yes," Helena said, "between want and ignorance, the second is far worse."

"Aye, miss. For want can end, but those who are ignorant are doomed."

Gracious, but for one so small, she was quite wise. Helena thought back to how the girl had watched over and guided her brother—her life had certainly forced her to grow up quickly. "I am glad you are able to find some refuge here at Hedgewood."

"'Tis better than prison," her voice shook a bit, "or the workhouses."

Indeed, even with the likes of a stern housekeeper to answer to, working here would be far better than the alternative. But she didn't like how their topic of conversation seemed to weigh the little girl down. "Tell me your brother's name."

"Jim, miss."

Mary and Jim. Simple, sweet names. They fit the children well. Nonetheless, Helena had not forgotten her mention of a Mr. Chant. The little thing was warming to her, but Helena thought it was quite possible she would close up quickly if Helena asked too many questions outright. "Have your parents left this earth, then?"

"Aye. Three years ago, it was. During winter, like this."

Helena's heart ached anew. "And is it only the two of you now?"

Mary didn't answer right away, but her steps slowed.

Perhaps asking directly was the only option open to Helena. "You mentioned a Mr. Chant. Is he your uncle?"

"Aye." The girl's expression, however, was at odds with her affirmation.

Whoever Mr. Chant was, he made Mary most uneasy. "Do you see him often?" By which Helena truly wanted to know if he hurt her and Jim often.

"Now and then."

Another half-truth, if Helena was correct in her assessment. Then again, it very well could be that Mary didn't like to speak about a man who regularly raised a hand to her and her brother.

At that moment, however, they reached the house.

Mary dropped into yet another curtsy; Helena had never seen someone curtsy as frequently as this little girl. "If there's nothing else, miss, I'll return to m' duties."

The girl was right; she did understand the ways of a big house. Helena hoped it would be enough to keep her and her brother inside for many winters to come.

"Thank you for walking with me, Mary."

With that, the little girl was gone, rushing off to see to laundry and dishes and who knew what else. Helena stood just outside the door for several minutes, staring at the footprints Mary had left behind in the snow. It felt good to have befriended a little girl who needed it. Perhaps if she applied herself, she could think up some other way to help them even more? Helena was alone in the world, with hardly a penny to her name, but that didn't mean she didn't intend to try. She still had friends, and she still had her wits. After speaking with Mary, she felt positively rich.

Moreover, she couldn't help but feel she'd been a bit pitiful as of late.

For the first time, Helena felt hopeful regarding the gentleman Lady Chapman had written. Lady Chapman said he was an upstanding, honorable man. It was wrong to demand more. She'd been richly blessed her whole life, in so many ways children like Mary and Jim would never be. From now on, she would focus less on her own situation and more on others. She would be less greedy and more generous. Life wasn't easy for anyone, yet she was determined, somehow, to make the most of her own.

CHAPTER FIFTEEN

The only benefit to finding himself tricked into walking into dinner with Miss Wynn was that it left a man time to carefully spy on one's sister while his dinner companion prattled on and on regarding lace, fashion, and the latest plates in *La Belle Assemblée*.

Fredrick nodded when he thought appropriate, but mostly his attention was on Christina. Both she and Eleanor had spent a great deal of time with Topper while on horseback that afternoon. Fredrick hadn't thought anything of it at the time. Now, though, Eleanor was sitting quite farther away at the table than the twins normally sat. Christina, moreover, seemed to speak to no one *but* Topper.

He was very likely being overly concerned. There was probably nothing between them other than friendship. After all, a lady could not always choose for herself who walked her into dinner, as Miss Wynn had somehow managed to do. Nor could she always choose to sit beside her sister. Nonetheless, Fredrick didn't miss the several glances Eleanor was giving Christina. Nor the fact that Christina didn't return a single one. He may be wrong—he certainly had been before when it came to his sisters—but he was growing more and more certain something had changed that afternoon.

"Do you not agree, Lord Chapman?"

Blast, what had Miss Wynn been saying? He was fairly sure it had been something about cream-colored lace being superior to ivory-colored lace.

"I suppose it depends on the dress and on the wearer."

Either he hadn't been following Miss Wynn's diatribe as closely as he'd hoped, or she simply didn't enjoy someone disagreeing with her. Either way, she turned away from him in a huff and began speaking to Lord Ellis, who sat on her other side.

Blessedly, at that same moment, Miss Spencer, who sat on his left, turned away from her own dinner partner, Lord Forbes.

Fredrick leaned slightly toward her. "What do you make of Christina just now?"

Miss Spencer's gaze moved from one twin to the other.

"She's the one with Topper," he offered.

Miss Spencer let out a small, gruff sigh. "I know that—or I would have had you given me just a minute longer to ascertain whose face is longer, and whose hair is a shade darker."

Fredrick smiled; he liked how determined she was to tell one from the other. Most people he knew remained content to lump his two sisters together and treat them as though they were one and the same. It drove Christina and Eleanor to madness frequently.

"She seems to be having a good time," Miss Spencer said.

Fredrick agreed; that wasn't what was bothering him. "Does she seem to be enjoying herself *too* much?"

Miss Spencer picked up her glass and took a sip, but he could see her watching his sister over the rim of her glass.

"Now that you mention it, she does seem rather . . . focused on her conversation with Topper."

Then he wasn't imagining things. His leg began to bounce slightly. What did he know of Topper, truly? Yes, Lady Andrews was known for inviting only the best lot to her house parties, but what respectable gentleman used that as reason to shirk his brotherly responsibilities? He would need to speak with Topper and—

Miss Spencer's hand brushed over his knee and rested against his leg. The touch was unexpected and wholly upending. Why Lord Ellis, Topper, and Lord Forbes weren't fawning over her by now, he couldn't rightly say.

"You're shaking the table," she whispered and slipped her hand away once more.

The light touch had sent pricks of awareness up his leg and heat up his neck. And yet, Fredrick found himself wishing she'd kept her hand there, regardless. He ground his jaw, forcing his gaze, and his thoughts, to remain on his sister. "You've spoken with Topper more than I have. What sort of man is he? Is he honorable?" He very well could be a cad—a jackanapes who only *acted* respectably in company.

"He has always been very polite."

"Might it be an act, though?" He knew far too many gentlemen who assumed one demeanor among the ladies of the *ton* and another entirely when in the gaming dens and worse.

"I suppose, but I saw no indication it was."

"But it *might* be."

Miss Spencer slowly lowered her fork onto the table and looked over at him. She had one eyebrow raised. "You seem determined to think ill of him."

"And if I am?"

"I would call it poor form."

He flattened his mouth into a tight line. "You said as much to me in the library."

"Perhaps that's what *I* always say when *you* are around." She plopped a bit of mutton into her mouth.

He leaned forward and began cutting his own mutton. "I cannot like all the attention he's giving her."

"Cannot or *will* not?"

Fredrick very nearly dropped his silverware in frustration. "And here I thought we were friends."

Miss Spencer had the audacity to giggle under her breath. "Of course we're friends. But Christina and I are friends as well. Don't you want to see her happily situated?"

"Yes. I suppose."

"As the one responsible for her, I would have thought you a little more eager to be rid of her," Miss Spencer teased.

Fredrick rocked his head to the side, eying her sideways. "So now I'm your *boorish* friend?"

She lifted her half-bare shoulder in a dainty shrug. The sight sent his heart into a strange, syncopated race.

"No, you are right," he said. "I *am* being boorish. And overprotective."

"You're a good brother."

"I don't know if I am. The problem is, I'm her *only* brother. I wish I knew what my father would have done in this situation. It's completely up to me to watch over her and Eleanor. To see that they make good matches. I always knew, growing up, that someday they would be courted and would eventually marry. I just never imagined *I* would be the one charged with the responsibility of seeing them properly settled."

"Is it a very heavy weight?"

Surprised at the question, Fredrick turned back toward her. Miss Spencer watched Christina and Topper, her tone sincere and her expression matched. She was curious, but there was also a hint of sadness in her eyes.

"Yes," he answered honestly. "I have found it to be weighty to the point of distress at times."

"There were nights, after balls or musicales, when my father would question me about this gentleman or that. Who had I spoken to? What had they said? How did I respond? He always looked . . . troubled, burdened during those conversations. I always wondered if it was me he was worried about, or—"

"The men you were keeping company with," Fredrick answered definitively. "Certainly, the men."

"I hope you are right. I hate the thought of him not trusting me or thinking me naive."

"I am certain he didn't." No one who knew Miss Spencer well at all would ever consider her naive or easily taken in by flattery. She was lighthearted and joyful but in no way gullible.

"How about this." Miss Spencer leaned a bit closer, keeping her voice low. "Since you and I are friends, what if I helped you keep an eye on Christina and Topper?"

The relief he felt at the very idea was so noticeable, he half expected to suddenly find himself an inch or two taller. "Have you any idea what a relief it will be to not do this alone?"

"I can fathom."

He was sure she could. After all, since her father had passed, she'd been seeing to many things alone. She'd packed up her childhood home, endured a London Season, and faced the derision of society. Yes, she had the Shakerleys. But after learning of Lord Shakerley's complete lack of brains in arranging her marriage contract, Fredrick doubted he'd helped her much with anything else.

"I can subtly bring up Topper's name after the ladies withdraw tonight," Miss Spencer said. "I will be able to watch them when you cannot. It may prove that Topper is more willing to speak with me regarding his intentions than he would to you, seeing as you are Christina's brother."

Fredrick was feeling far more optimistic already. "That would be much appreciated." He could use an astute head like hers in sorting all this out. And heaven knew, between his mother and twin sisters, he had plenty of 'sorting out' to do.

CHAPTER SIXTEEN

Helena moved through the grand doors and into a ballroom as beautifully decorated as any she'd ever seen.

Lord Forbes, standing beside her, let out a low whistle even as his walking stick clicked lightly against the floor.

"It is quite grand, isn't it?" she agreed in a low whisper. Ribbons hung in lovely curls down table legs and in the gathers of the tablecloths. The entire ceiling was draped in sheer tulle, making the many candelabras which burned above them appear to be shimmering, light-giving clouds. Flowers—nearly an entire hothouse's worth—filled corners and tables and surrounded the orchestra at one side of the room.

"I'd heard Lady Adley rather went all out for Christmas," Lord Forbes said in a rare show of actual emotion, "but I had no idea."

"I think it's lovely," Emma said from behind them, her hand atop Topper's arm.

Lord Forbes led Helena further into the room. "Lord Adley must love his wife quite a lot to let her spend so much of his blunt on a Christmas ball."

Helena's forehead dropped a bit at his comment. Lord Forbes's statement had been straightforward enough, but something about it had given her pause. No doubt she would have dismissed it out of hand had she not been thinking all evening if he might not be the answer to her problems.

Did Lord Forbes not think a ball a good reason to decorate? Or that a man only gave a woman he *loved* money to see her wishes fulfilled? Or, perhaps, his tastes were simply more reserved, and he perceived the room they stood in as unnecessarily extravagant?

Lord Chapman entered the room, Christina on his right arm and Eleanor on his left. Helena watched his eyes grow big as he took in the space. Then his gaze found hers and he mouthed, "Extraordinary." She smiled back at him and nodded her agreement. Lady Adley, whom Helena was determined she ought to meet tonight, had certainly a fine talent for seeing a ballroom merrily decorated.

Moreover, she was not here to tease out a single, insignificant sentence from Lord Forbes. She was here to enjoy herself, to meet people, and possibly to further her connection with a gentleman or two. What Lord Forbes might have meant was of little concern. Helena could feel her spirits rising the more she soaked in the jolly atmosphere of the ballroom.

When Lord Forbes asked her to dance not five minutes later, Helena readily agreed. Dancing, she learned, was ever so much more fun when the room was filled with red and green decorations and the orchestra played lively and heartily. After the dance ended, and Lord Forbes excused himself, Helena spoke with Emma and a couple of her friends whom she hadn't yet met. Then she danced with Topper, and afterward, he brought her some punch. As the evening wore on, Helena found herself in such a fine mood, she even agreed to dance with Lord Ellis when he asked her. More still, she hardly cared when he spent more time looking at the women beside her than he did at her.

At least he had the decency to see her comfortably situated on a well-cushioned chair near a window before he left. She didn't care for his good opinion, so his lack of attention did little to disappoint her.

Helena closed her eyes for a moment, reveling in the cheerful ambiance surrounding her. Still, she didn't miss the sound of a chair being pushed up beside hers and of someone sitting down heavily onto it.

"He's dancing with her *again.*"

She didn't have to open her eyes to know who'd spoken, and she couldn't help but smile. "Really, Lord Chapman, if you've come with the intent on ruining my good mood, you will find me a very unwilling partner."

"Tell as much to Topper."

Helena opened her eyes and glanced his way. Lord Chapman seemed ready to demand Topper remove himself from the ball altogether.

"This is only the second time he's asked her to dance," she said. "That may be proof he is interested, but it doesn't make him a cad."

Lord Chapman's gaze followed Christina and Topper across the dance floor; clearly, she hadn't convinced him. She'd already spoken to Christina enough to learn of her good opinion of Topper, and all her interactions with him had only shown him to be a gentleman. However, she'd already told Lord Chapman as much and didn't think repeating herself now would make any difference.

"If he likes her, then I wish nothing but the best for them."

"You aren't her brother."

"No, I'm not. But if you aren't careful, pretty soon Christina's going to wish I *was* and you were not."

Lord Chapman's gaze shifted to her and he stared at her

long and hard. Then his shell broke and his mouth shifted into a smile. "You are right. He's shown no signs of wanting to misuse her, and he is well enough off. I doubt he's a fortune hunter. I should just sit back"—he did so even as he spoke, folding his arms across his chest—"and not bother them."

"Good for you." Helena turned her own gaze back to the dance, her shoulder nearly brushing his as she shifted in her chair. A comfortable silence settled between them. Despite it, Helena could feel Lord Chapman's intent gaze stretching out and landing on Topper.

"You're still going to keep a close eye on him though, aren't you?" she asked, already knowing the answer.

"As close as a saddle on a horse's back."

Helena pursed her lips and shook her head but didn't look his way. "Lord Chapman, you are incorrigible. I can't help but believe that someday when you meet the right woman, you will find yourself dancing with her twice during a single ball. And probably wishing you could dance a third time, too."

She turned to see what he thought of that and found herself staring back into his eyes. He looked at her, something different than she'd ever seen before swirling about his expression. His eyes looked darker just then; how could that be? And it was as though he was pulling on her, drawing her closer to him, even though he wasn't touching her at all. Helena's stomach turned into a hundred butterflies, all of them beating their wings against her chest.

"Lord Chapman," a happy voice called to them.

Lord Chapman looked away, and the spell was broken.

"Lord Adley," he said, standing and reaching a hand out to greet the newcomer. "It is good to see you, sir."

Helena realized that she'd been leaning quite close to him, and she righted herself. What had just happened?

Lord Chapman spoke easily enough with Lord Adley, and Helena was grateful for a moment to compose herself. Soon, however, Lord Chapman introduced her to their host. He was a short man, and a bit bald, but had a pleasing expression.

"You have a lovely home," Helena said, thankful that as a lady she was free to remain sitting. She wasn't at all confident she would be able to stand just now. "And it seems tonight is quite the success."

Lord Adley chuckled. "Between you and me, my wife was ever so worried that a ball the day *after* St. Nicolas would be seen as terribly unfashionable. But we have our own family tradition on St. Nicolas that none of us wanted to give up. So, here we are."

Helena's gaze floated over the crush around them. "It seems the gamble was worth it," she said. Her father and she had once had many Christmastime traditions. But they'd all ended with his death. Gracious, but she missed those moments. It wasn't the tradition themselves that were important, but the anticipation, the knowledge that they'd do them together this year and next year and the year after, just as they'd done them together so many years before.

Suddenly, Helena felt tears prick against the back of her eyes. Good heavens, she could not be seen crying at a ball. She blinked quickly and forced her mind back to the conversation about her.

Lord Adley indicated to the room in general with his glass of punch. "I had hoped to see Lord Wilkins tonight. I understand he's back from America with his cousin, Mr. Radcliff." Lord Adley leaned in a bit closer. "And I hear he's brought a proper American heiress back with him."

"I wish him all the best of luck, then," Lord Chapman said even as he eyed Helena. He seemed to be asking if she was all right.

Lord Adley shrugged. "He sent his apologies; apparently his mother has a rather bad headache."

"That is most unfortunate," Helena said, giving Lord

Chapman a small smile. She was fine, if suddenly a bit melancholy. Somewhere, moreover, she hoped Lord Wilkins—whomever he may be—was happy with his American heiress. Perhaps his cousin, Mr. Radcliff, too, could find someone to be happy with. Though she was alone this Christmas, it was nice to think that, somewhere, there were men and women happily celebrating together.

The sounds of the orchestra announcing the next set reached them.

"Pardon me," Lord Chapman said, reaching his hand out to Helena even while speaking to Lord Adley, "But I had hoped to ask Miss Spencer to honor me with this dance."

"Of course, of course." Lord Adley smiled at Helena good-naturedly. Then he stopped and turned toward the music. "Good gracious, is it the midnight waltz already? I must go find my wife." With a quick bow, he hurried off.

Helena slipped her hand into Lord Chapman's. Warmth spread down her arm. It was as though he'd poured comforting reassurance into her with a simple touch. Truth was, she wasn't wholly alone this Christmas; she couldn't ever remember feeling lonely when with Lord Chapman, though she felt it often enough around other people.

Together, they moved toward the center of the ballroom. Several other couples pushed past them, hurrying to join in what was quickly becoming the largest dance of the night. Helena knew a moment of gratitude for the crush which enveloped them and the resulting invisibility.

"Remembering your father again?" Lord Chapman asked in a whisper, his mouth close to her ear.

Helena nodded. "As I told you before, sometimes it just hits me. Though I must admit, it seems to happen around you more often than anyone else."

He placed a hand against the small of her back, gently guiding her. "You never have to hide your tears from me."

Helena blinked more tears away. Heaven help her, but sometimes no matter what she tried, she couldn't stop them. Helena's steps slowed. Lord Chapman must have understood for he didn't press her to continue. Instead, they came to a halt just outside the gathering dance.

"Does it bother you?" Helena asked, her voice low enough that only he would hear.

"Does what bother me?"

Her voice grew even quieter. "How short life is?"

Instead of responding, he merely leaned in closer, his hand still against her back, his fingers tracing small circles there.

What was it about his presence that always made her feel so secure? So safe voicing those fears she didn't dare tell anyone else? "Sometimes I can't help but feel it's all so pointless," she said. "We're babies, then children, then adults, and soon we're in the grave. One minute here, the next gone. It all feels so frightfully short."

"I guess we just have to make the most of the time we're given."

The dance began, and couples swirled across the floor in front of them. Helena watched, but it was the feel of Lord Chapman beside her that she mostly focused on. "But how does one even begin to do that? How do I even know if I *am* doing that?" Despite her better judgment, she leaned her shoulder against his chest. She wished she could lean her head against his shoulder, but they were at a ball and easily seen by all. Still, the bit of touch brought the comfort she needed. "After my father passed away, my world changed in many ways. One of those ways is that I cannot shake the feeling that someday I'm going to die, too. What if I pass on without having seen to those matters most important? What if I die with work left undone?"

"And what work do you feel you must do?"

"I don't know." Her gaze traveled across the faces of those

dancing and smiling, seemingly oblivious to the fact that very soon, this would all end for them. Though, perhaps they were less oblivious and simply distracted by the night's merriment. "I've been so focused on finding a husband. But now—" She turned and faced him fully, her tone still soft but intense. "I want more than just an advantageous connection. I want a *family*. I want someone who cares for me, and someone I can care for in return. I want children whom we'll love. And then . . ." She drew herself up, Mary and Jim's faces coming to mind. "Then I also want to help other people. I want to be looking beyond my own silly worries, and I want to help those who are muddling through life at the same time I am. I don't know how or whom, but I know I want to be helping others."

His gaze held hers with equal intensity. "Then do it."

She shook her head. "I don't know where to start." It had seemed so simple after speaking with Mary the other day. She had much, and others had less. If only she could help those less blessed than her. But now, after spending much time these past few days thinking it over, she didn't know the first place to begin. In many ways, the despair was worse than ever. Not only could she do very little to help herself, but she couldn't think of any way to help others in a meaningful way. What a useless waste her life was proving to be.

"If I've learned anything about you this Christmas, Miss Spencer, it's that you're thoughtful and persistent. You'll figure it out." His hand cupped her cheek with a gloved hand. The touch was comfortable and easy, yet it also brought a heat to her chest that she'd never felt before. The music and dancers, the decorations and chalked floors, they all faded away around them. All she could see was Lord Chapman, smiling at her and standing ever so close.

"Just start where you are," he said. "You don't have to do anything monumental. Just make a difference in the lives of those you meet every day." He didn't pull back, and one corner of his lips tipped upward. His voice dropped to a whisper. "I think we missed joining the dance."

Helena laughed softly.

"Poor form?" he asked, slowly pulling his hand away from her face.

"Indubitably," she said, turning and once more seeing the ball around them. Helena drew in a deep breath—no friend had ever comforted her like that. She both yearned for it and was wholly unsure of what she was feeling. Her insides were a jumbled mess, yet she wasn't uncomfortable. She felt at peace, especially when her thoughts returned to her father and her desire to help others, yet she also felt wholly unbalanced.

Lord Chapman took hold of her hand and looped it around his arm. "You deserve a family," he said. "You deserve a man who will cherish you."

His sincere tone pulled her gaze to him. He stood shoulder to shoulder with her, watching the dancers. He was as dear a friend to her as any she'd ever had—how that had come about, or when, she couldn't rightly say. But, standing together, she knew it now. More alarming, however, was a growing heat in her chest which bespoke of him being more to her than just a friend.

It was an emotion Helena had never experienced before and one she had no idea how to handle. She couldn't feel this way for Lord Chapman. He was the man who'd flatly refused to marry her only last summer.

If ever she was in need of a family to help her sort out life, it was now.

CHAPTER SEVENTEEN

Helena hurried down the stairs, grateful that no one else was up yet. Last night's Christmas ball had been an emotional whirlwind, one she was still sifting through. The magic which had captivated her, the heartache at missing her father once more, the realization that she'd changed somewhere along the way and didn't want to sit back and miss opportunities to help other people, the heat which had come from Lord Chapman's touch.

Heavens, when she listed out all the things she'd experienced in a single night, she was rather amazed she was able to pull herself out of bed at all.

After the dance, after she'd retired to bed and lain awake for some time trying to make sense of it all, she'd come to a conclusion and hadn't been able to shake it when she'd first awoken that morning.

She was done waiting for her uncle to write.

Helena wanted—needed—her family. Nothing was more important to her. That included her mother's memory, the traditions she and her father had shared, and whether he liked it or not, it included Uncle Scrooge. Helena reached the entryway and checked her reflection in the mirror. Her bonnet was secure, and her hair seemed safely tucked inside. Her face was a bit drawn, perhaps, hardly surprising since she'd been out late last night and up again early this morning. The butler passed and Helena requested he have a horse saddled for her.

"Perhaps the tan one, Starfire?"

The butler's eyebrow ticked up a bit. "I would advise against it. Starfire is quite difficult to manage, even for the master. But I will see to it that a proper mount is brought around."

"Very well." She'd have to tackle riding the headstrong horse another day.

"Will you be wanting a footman to accompany you, miss?" the butler asked.

"Yes, thank you."

With a bow, he moved off.

Helena was left with nothing to do but wring her hands until the horse was brought around. What was she to say to Uncle Scrooge? How did one begin a conversation with a man who seemed content to remain strangers? Suppose he refused to see her at all?

"Are you going somewhere this morning, Miss Spencer?"

Helena turned to find Christina coming down the stairs, dressed becomingly in a lovely primrose morning gown.

"I'm just off to town to see to a small matter of business."

"I see." Christina reached the bottom of the stairs and hurried up to Helena. "Actually, I'm glad I've found you. I feel I need to speak with you . . . about something."

Christina glanced about, her hands fidgeting. Helena couldn't imagine what Christina was so scared to say. She reached out and placed a hand on Christina's arm. "We have become quite good friends. You know you can tell me anything."

Christina smiled at the reassurance, but it didn't qualm the agitation in her eyes. "First, I want to say that I didn't mean for anything to happen. Emma, Eleanor, myself—we all agreed that this Christmas was going to be about finding *you* a husband. You need it so much more than any of us."

"Is this about Topper?"

Christina took hold of Helena's hand tightly. "I promise, I was only trying to help you. I thought if I feigned a headache the other day during our ride, everyone would just stay and listen to you. But then he rode back with me and, oh, Helena, he is so considerate. And we love all the same books and when he takes my hand—" She ended with an intense sigh that conveyed more than words.

Helena couldn't help but smile. "If he is all that, then I am happy for you."

"Truly? I have been ever so cast down, thinking you must hate me." Christina stood up straighter and held Helena's gaze with a sincere, intense one of her own—apparently Lord Chapman was not the only member of his family who knew how to do that. "Tell me honestly. Are you upset?"

Helena searched her own emotions but could not find any disappointment or regret. "I am in earnest. I only wish you two the best."

Christina squealed, her hands clasping at her chest. "Thank you."

Helena *did* find herself curious, though. "I must ask, are things settled between you two?"

Christina pinkened. "Oh, no. Nothing so far as all that. But . . . last night, we danced twice, and then he stayed and spoke with me nearly the whole night. La, Helena, it was heavenly."

Helena could feel her own smile tugging hard against her cheeks. How could one not be elated when a friend was so happy?

A footman approached and informed her that two horses

had been brought around and saddled, and that he would be accompanying her.

"Thank you . . ."

"Willis, if you please, miss."

"Thank you, Willis. If you'll wait just a minute, I am ready."

He bowed and moved off to give her some privacy.

Helena turned back to Christina and wrapped her in a hug. "I hope he makes you happy."

Christina squeezed her in return. "I believe he shall."

"I'll warn you, though," Helena said before letting go. "Your brother has been fit to be tied watching him court you."

"Oh, Fredrick is nothing but a big puppy," Christina said. "He growls a lot but is soft as butter on the inside."

With another hug, Helena left her friend smiling in the entryway and followed Willis out the door. The same horse she'd ridden the other day was waiting for her with a sidesaddle. Making use of the mounting block which had also been brought around, Helena was soon ready to leave. But her thoughts didn't drift far.

Emma would no doubt be less than thrilled to learn that Christina and Topper had formed a connection. Helena, for her part, couldn't find it in herself to be anything less than elated for her friend. Topper, too, was a good man and deserved so kind a wife as the one he would find in Christina.

The real question was, what would Lord Chapman say? The thought of speaking with him brought a heat to her face. Why was she reacting so, even to the mere thought of him? Helena shook off the nonsense.

For now, she needed to focus on her uncle. What he would say or do when she unexpectedly showed up at his place of business, she could not imagine. But as one big puppy had reminded her last night, she deserved family. And right now, the only family she had was about to find her unwilling to silently walk away.

FREDRICK WATCHED FROM HIS BEDCHAMBER WINDOW AS HELENA mounted her horse and rode off, a footman following after. Even after she'd rounded the bend and was well out of sight, his eyes refused to turn away. Gads, but attending the ball last night had proven a monumental mistake.

The sheer curtain slipped from his fingers and fell back into place between him and the window. With a grumble, he finally forced himself away from the snowy view and turned back toward his room. He'd been so convinced that the warmth of Helena's touch would fade. It had only been a shock the first time she'd unexpectedly rested her hand against his arm—a shock, and that was all. He had convinced himself that all the other times, the heat was growing less and that soon he would know her so well as to look at her as he did either Christina or Eleanor.

Convinced himself? Ha. Deluded himself was more accurate.

He collapsed into a chair by the hearth and, resting his elbows against his legs, dropped his head into his upturned hands. Holding Helena's face in his hand last night had changed everything.

First off, he was suddenly struggling to think of her as 'Miss Spencer.' She hadn't given him permission to use her given name, nor was she likely to do so. But cupping her face in his hand, looking into her tear-rimmed eyes, seeing her ardent desire to help others and to make a family for herself again—

Blast, even reliving the memory was intoxicating.

Resting back against the chair, he kicked his feet out and

folded his arms. The real question was, what was he going to do now?

There was no going back. He knew as surely as he breathed that he was falling in love with Miss Helena Spencer.

And what of her feelings? After all he'd put her through, he should feel grateful she had ever deigned talk to him, but in no circumstance should he ever dare hope for more. She was too bright a woman to be caught up in a moment, an ardent look, the feel of someone standing so near one could smell the rosewater in her hair.

Fredrick shut his eyes, wishing the memory of last night would leave him alone.

He needed to stay focused on the truth. And the truth was, he'd not once caught her looking back at him the same way he knew he was looking at her. He'd not heard her breath catch when he reached out to her. She'd not blushed at his compliments nor vied for his attention. After several London Seasons, Fredrick felt he was fairly good at knowing when a woman was flirting with him. Helena had never, not once, flirted.

Perhaps that was why he was so drawn to her.

It was possible. Even likely. But he knew it was far more than that, though. He was drawn to her cheerful disposition and her willingness to find reasons to be happy despite having endured a very difficult year. He was drawn to her desire to help others, to see past her own sorrows. He was drawn to the way she smiled even when crying and to the obvious love she'd had for her father.

There were so many things he loved about her.

And that was a very real problem.

Avoiding her seemed like his best—possibly his only—course of action. The urge to be near her, to consider becoming hers forever, was always stronger the closer he was to her. If she returned to dressing like a lady's companion, that would certainly help. But that was not going to happen, he was sure. Why did Helena have to be so deucedly beautiful?

He hated the thought of staying away, but it would be for the best. Still, he wished he could do something for her. She'd been quite clearly overwrought last night. What could he do, or give her, to help ease some of her grief?

He stood and took to pacing. Holding her close was tempting; after all, she had leaned into him last night as she had spoken of her desires and heartache. But that would be what *he* wanted. And it would probably spell disaster. It had taken all of his effort to not kiss her last night.

Kiss her!

Gads, he was in trouble.

A new thought entered and with it a bolt of energy. A harp. That was what he could get for her. Lady Andrews had mentioned she had one in storage. Helena had seemed quite disappointed at not being able to play several weeks ago. If she was anything like Eleanor, playing music would ease some of her sadness.

She was gone at the moment, too. Which meant he was at no risk of running into her if he sought out Lord Andrews this morning. Striding purposefully, he made it through the door and down the corridor quickly. He might not be able to do much for Helena, but he felt hopeful that in this one small way, he could bring her comfort.

CHAPTER EIGHTEEN

Helena slowly walked up the small path which connected the street to the rickety old door. Her uncle's place of employment looked far worse than she'd imagined. The slats in the wooden door were breaking apart and were pocked with large holes. Why didn't the man have the thing repaired? The few whispered conversations she'd happened to overhear as a child all led her to believe that Uncle Scrooge was very successful; surely he could afford to fix a single door.

Then again, it well could be that the imaginings she'd drummed up regarding her uncle were a far cry from the truth.

Lifting a hand, she knocked heavily on the door. Willis stood a little behind her, silently watching. What would Uncle Scrooge say when she told him who she was? What kind of a scene would Willis end up reporting to the other servants at Hedgewood Manor? There was a sound of feet shuffling, and then the door slowly creaked open. An elderly man stood before Helena, his snowy white hair disheveled. Surely this was not Uncle Scrooge. Her uncle was only a few years older than her mother, not a few *decades* older, as this man appeared to be.

"I am here to see Mr. Scrooge," she said, hoping she wasn't about to offend the one and only family member she had living.

The elderly man smiled all the more, bowing. "Yes, please come in. Right this way. Right this way."

Helena followed the man inside and knew a brief moment of relief. At least she'd assumed correctly that this elderly, smiling man was not her uncle. The hallway she stepped into was far darker than she'd anticipated. It seemed, along with not having money for a door, her uncle didn't see the need to spend money on candles either. Or, perhaps he preferred the dark? Gracious, but it was unnerving to realize how little she knew about her only remaining relative.

"I am Mr. Cratchit," the elderly man said. He pointed off to the room on Helena's right. "Mr. Scrooge is in there." He offered Helena another smile and bow. "Now, if you'll excuse me, I have many things to see to." With no more than that, he left her standing in the hallway.

The elderly man had not asked Helena's name nor had he announced her. That left the divulging of who she truly was all on Helena's shoulders.

She took a small step toward the dark room. She could not ever recall having seen her uncle. Father had mentioned once or twice that Uncle Scrooge used to join them for this celebration or that. But the rift which ran deep between Uncle Scrooge and the rest of the family had been well-etched even before Helena was out of leading strings.

A man sat behind a wide, old desk. Of a truth, all the furniture in the space looked as old and worn out as the front door. Did the man never repair anything? Helena walked directly up to the desk, trying hard not to wring her hands. But Uncle Scrooge did not look up. He remained bent over, quill in one hand, furiously scribbling on what appeared to be a financial ledger.

Helena stood silent for several minutes, awaiting acknowledgment, aware of Willis waiting patiently in the hallway behind her. The only sound in the room was the scratch of pen against paper, and that was only broken by the occasional sound of a pen tapping against the glass ink bottle.

Well, if Mother's brother was unwilling to begin the conversation, she would have to.

"Hello, Uncle."

The pen scratching stopped. The man stilled, his gaze not lifting higher than the paper before him.

Did this man remember her at all? Helena extended a hand. "I am Miss Helena Spencer, Fanny's daughter—"

"I know who you are." His voice was gruff and gravelly.

Well, at least she didn't need to explain her parentage. She waited for Uncle Scrooge to say more, but the man didn't offer another word.

After a drawn-out moment, Helena motioned toward the questionable-looking chair to her right. "May I?"

Uncle Scrooge let out a gruff grunt. "If you must."

No doubt that was as elegant an invitation to sit she was ever going to receive. The chair squeaked as she sat, and for a moment, Helena wasn't fully sure it would support her. But the sad piece of furniture didn't collapse—that was one good thing that had happened so far this visit.

If only Lord Chapman was here. His presence had the uncanny ability to calm her and set her at ease. She could use a bit of that just now. Her stomach was aflutter and her nerves on edge.

"Why are you here?" Uncle Scrooge asked.

Helena opened her mouth to explain. But how did one explain that she missed having family? How did one ask someone so gruff if they wouldn't mind *being* that family after so many years of not knowing each other?

"I'd like to invite you to dinner on Christmas Day," Helena

said. She hadn't exactly talked it over with Lady Andrews. However, she felt sure, if she explained who Scrooge was, her host wouldn't mind too terribly. Moreover, even if it was a horrible breach of propriety, she needed her uncle.

"You've come to ask to borrow money," Uncle Scrooge said, still not bothering to look up.

Helena's eyes widened, and she only just caught her jaw from dropping open. "No, sir, that isn't—"

"You are an orphan and unmarried. I was not your father's man of business, but I knew enough of his estate to be fully aware that it was entailed away. That will have left you with only your dowry—a quaint sum, if I'm not mistaken, hardly an amount to be proud of. Moreover, you will not have access to it currently as you do not reach your majority for another year yet."

Helena was shocked into silence. Slowly her uncle lifted his head. Helena didn't know what she had expected—she couldn't remember her mother and only had two small likenesses of her. But this man, with his deep wrinkles and perpetual scowl, was not at all how she'd imagined her mother's brother to be.

"Therefore, I can assume that you are," he said, "penniless for the time being. Having had no family and no offers these past fourteen"—he paused momentarily—"no, nearer fifteen months, you are reaching the end of what pin money you had stored away before your father's unexpected death. And so you reach out to me for a loan." His tone turned toward more of a mutter as he finished, almost to himself. "You would have been wiser to save more before finding yourself alone."

Helena could do no more than breathe for nearly a full minute. *This* was her uncle? *This* was the man who'd been a brother to her beloved mother and was now her closest living relation?

"Excuse me, but I did not come to see you about money,

Uncle Scrooge." She was struggling to form even the most rudimentary words.

"*Mister* Scrooge will do just fine."

Good heavens, this was far colder a reception than she'd anticipated, even during her most blue-deviled moments. "Very well, *Mr.* Scrooge." Helena drew herself up. "Despite what you clearly believe, I have come solely for the purpose of beginning afresh between us. This time of year, more than any other, I believe is a time for setting aside past hurts and wrongs, and for reconnecting with family and those we hold dear."

"Humbug."

She would not be gainsaid so easily. "Please come. We will have a jolly dinner and plenty of games of wit afterward."

Uncle Scrooge—for such Helena would still *think* of him—huffed. "Keep Christmas in your own way and let me keep it in mine."

"But you don't keep it."

"Let me leave it alone then."

He could not truly wish to be so miserly. Uncle Scrooge may *think* he wanted his life to be depressing, but deep down, Helena had to believe there was a heart in there, somewhere.

When she didn't respond right away, Uncle Scrooge muttered, "What reason have you to make yourself merry? You've admitted to being poor."

"What reason have you to be miserable? You've admitted to being rich."

"Bah, I've never admitted to any such thing."

"But you can afford to loan money to the entire neighborhood, or so I've been told. That loan money must originate somewhere."

"Do you want my money or a discussion on philosophy? If it be the second, I recommend the pub down the street. If it be the first, I suggest you shut your trap."

Helena rocked back in her chair, embarrassment flaming

against her cheeks, both from his cutting words as well as his harsh tone.

Willis stalked forward. "Need I remind you, sir, you are speaking to a lady." His words were hard, and Helena caught sight of his curled fist at his side.

Helena stood, swallowing hard. It seemed the time had come to leave. "It's all right, Willis," she said, nonetheless grateful that he would speak up for her. She turned back to her uncle. "The invitation to Christmas Day dinner still stands."

"Bah."

Helena set her jaw and turned away. "Come, Willis, I believe it is time we leave."

CHAPTER NINETEEN

The ride back to Hedgewood Manor did little to calm Helena.

How dare that man speak to her like that. Had he no compassion, no kindness in his heart at all? She'd always secretly wondered if her grandfather wasn't mostly to blame for the rift between them. Now, however, she wondered that Mother cared to keep in contact with her brother at all.

Of all the rude, inconsiderate, brutish responses.

She dismounted quickly once they arrived and hurried into the house. She needed time to herself—or perhaps a conversation with Lord Chapman. He would understand.

Helena pulled off her bonnet and pelisse then hurried down the corridor, checking each room as she passed. Lady Andrews sat in the drawing room with Miss Wynn and Lady Chapman. In the parlor, she found Lord Ellis and Lord Andrews laughing over a bottle of port. She checked the library next, but only found Eleanor, Christina, Lord Forbes and Topper. No Lord Chapman.

Not caring that she was scowling, Helena stomped toward her bedchamber.

"Helena, wait."

She paused at the sound of Eleanor's voice but didn't turn.

Eleanor caught up to her quickly. "Fredrick said he had business to see to all day, but he left you something."

"Oh?" Helena's shoulders lifted a bit.

"This way." Eleanor looped her arm through Helena's. "It's in the music room."

Helena allowed herself to be led back down the stairs. When she entered the room, her breath caught.

Standing in the center of the room was a most elegant harp. Two maids were running cloths over the instrument; it most likely had only just been pulled out of storage.

"Isn't it beautiful?" Eleanor giggled. "Fredrick spoke to Lord Andrews over breakfast this morning."

It *was* beautiful. Helena walked up to the tall instrument and placed her hand lightly against it. How many months had gone by since she'd last played? The Shakerleys didn't have a harp, and her own had been part of her father's estate, which meant she'd had to give it up soon after his passing.

The maids both curtsied and hurried out of the room. Helena pulled over the stool that she guessed they had brought down with the harp. She sat but did no more than run her fingers over the instrument.

"Well, play something," Eleanor encouraged.

Helena took hold of the harp and rested it against her shoulder. The feel was wonderful. How she'd missed this. Lifting her hands, she brushed her fingers over the strings. The sound was lovely. Clear, but not too sharp.

"This is a very nice instrument," she said.

"No doubt, but I think I'd like it even more if you actually played something."

Helena shot Eleanor a glare, but she couldn't truly be upset. Fredrick had seen to it that she had exactly what she needed to get hold of herself after her trying morning meeting Uncle Scrooge.

FREDRICK STOOD, HIS BACK PRESSED AGAINST THE WALL. Blessedly, the corridor was empty save himself. He'd hate to have to explain why he was standing *outside* the music room when all the other guests were chatting cheerfully *inside*.

Helena laughed, the sound carrying out of the room. It pulled on him, beckoning him to join the others. But he wouldn't. Even being this close to her was proving dangerous; he wouldn't risk actually being in the same room she was, not after catching sight of how becoming she was in blue.

Music reached him next. Helena had begun playing again. The song was lovely. Fredrick pressed his head against the wall behind him. He'd been confident when he'd asked Lord Andrews to pull out the harp for her that he was doing the right thing. He was doing a *safe* thing. Only now did he realize how wrong he had been. He never dreamed anyone could play so beautifully. It was nearly too much for him. He ached to march in there and sit directly beside her. Perhaps even place his hand against the small of her back as she played.

He would listen. Smile. Wait for her to smile up at him.

See the light in her eyes.

"Fredrick?"

He stood up straight and whirled around.

Mother stood beside him in her ever-present matte black. He hadn't even heard her leave the music room.

"Whatever are you doing out here?" she asked, rightfully perplexed.

Punishing myself.

"Nothing. Just thinking through a few estate problems," he fibbed.

"In the corridor?" she said, one eyebrow raised.

Fredrick ran a hand over the back of his neck. He didn't want to discuss this with his mother, but neither could he think up a suitable excuse.

"Never mind," she hurried on. "You can set aside your *problems* for now—"

Just how much of his current predicament did Mother understand? She was giving him a terribly knowing look.

"—and join me in the entryway. I have heard that your Uncle Baker has just arrived."

"Uncle Baker?" Whatever was he doing here?

Mother brushed past him, waving for him to follow. Fredrick dutifully fell in line but missed the sound of Helena's playing the moment they were out of earshot.

"I did not know my uncle would be joining us this Christmas," he said as they neared the entryway. Through the grand windows on either side of the door, he could see a carriage and people bustling about. But no one had entered the house yet.

"That is entirely my fault, you know," Mother said, not a hint of remorse in her voice. "You have been so terribly occupied with business matters, I thought you might appreciate another gentleman's advice. Lady Andrews assured me another couple of guests would be no trouble at all."

Why ever would he want *more* advice? He didn't say so to Mother—he had been raised never to disrespect her—but if he truly had estate questions he could have asked Lord Andrews or even Lord Shakerley. Baker hardly even saw to any of his own estate problems; Father had always handled those things. If anything, Baker should be wanting to see *him* with questions regarding his own estate.

The door burst open and Baker and Fredrick's cousin, Alice, tumbled into the room. With many shouts and 'haloo!'s they all greeted one another. The housekeeper asked if either Baker or Alice cared to rest after their journey. Fredrick wasn't the least bit surprised when they both chose not to, declaring instead that they wished to meet all the other guests.

Not ten minutes after Fredrick had trudged downstairs, the four of them were moving back toward the music room.

Alice fell back a pace to speak with Fredrick's mother while Baker talked at a furious rate about the many wonders he'd seen in Dover that autumn.

"Most gentlemen go north for the hunting," he said as they stepped into the music room. "But I say, go south. Avoid the crowds. Enjoy the warmer—"

Baker's diatribe ceased suddenly. Unsure what had caused the unusual silence, Fredrick turned his way.

And found Baker staring directly at Helena, his mouth agape.

Ah, blast, Mother had probably forgotten to tell Baker that the woman he'd tried to get Fredrick to marry was here—the very woman who'd experienced much hardship thanks to Baker and Shakerley's meddling machinations. Well, he hoped his uncle felt good and sorry for what he'd done. A bit of guilt wouldn't hurt him in the least.

However, as he studied Uncle further, a tinge of unease skittered through him. The expression on Uncle's face was not one of guilt or even embarrassment.

Lady Andrews stood and hurried over, and introductions were quickly made. All the while, Baker hardly took his eyes off of Helena.

"Pardon me, Lady Andrews," he said when first there was a lull in the conversation, "but who is that ravishing woman there? The one who was playing the harp when we entered?"

"Oh?" Lady Andrews turned about as though expecting someone besides Helena to be at the harp. "That is Miss Spencer. Would you care for an introduction?"

"Yes, please."

Baker's voice was far too eager for Fredrick's taste. His

stomach clenched tightly as Baker walked away with Lady Andrews.

Alice sidled up close to Fredrick. "Perhaps I should warn you. It appears Papa has finally gotten over Mother's death. He has been on the hunt, as you might say, these past three months."

Great. This was just what he needed. His own uncle making eyes at Helena.

"She's a little young for him, don't you think?" Alice said, listing her head. "But then, my good friend Margret married a man three years Papa's senior and she, two months younger than I am. I suppose it is not all that strange."

Fredrick could have sworn the voices around him were growing muffled, and the floor was rocking slightly beneath his boots. This was absurd. Unthinkable.

Alice moved forward, joining her father near the harp and engaging Helena in conversation. The two of them seemed about ready to overwhelm Helena, and she glanced more than once over at Fredrick. Each time, her attention was immediately demanded by her new acquaintances.

"What do you think?" Mother said, moving up beside him.

That he was suddenly hating this day. That he couldn't seem to make sense of his life anymore. He sighed. "What do I think about what?"

Mother tutted. "Of *them*. Of Miss Spencer and your uncle."

Gads, she was already speaking of them as a done deal. What the devil? Baker had only arrived a quarter of an hour ago.

"Oh, don't look at me like that," Mother said. "You might as well know. Helena herself came to Lady Shakerley and me, quite upset she was, and when I offered to help . . . arrange . . . something for her, she readily agreed."

So this *was* a done deal? "She came to you?" His gaze

moved back toward the harp. Helena was playing again, Baker smiling on. "She asked for help in . . .?" He waved a hand in her direction.

"Help in securing her future. Yes. Really, Fred, I don't see why this is so hard for you to swallow. The girl is a dear and has been through far too much already. Her only chance at a happy life is to marry and move past all you did to her this summer."

All *he'd* done? And what of Baker? Surely his uncle held some of the blame, too. But, no. Baker was the one who was going to marry Helena—at Helena's request, no less.

Watching Lord Ellis or even Lord Forbes vie for a conversation with Helena was torture enough—now this? Baker may be a decent man, but he was also a bit ridiculous.

Surely Helena would never . . .

Someone as astute as she couldn't possibly prefer . . .

Fredrick had to leave before he did something disgraceful. He'd been unsure of Helena's feelings toward him. Now, they were far too clear.

Without another word to Mother or anyone, Fredrick spun on his heel and marched out of the room.

CHAPTER TWENTY

Helena pulled hard on Starfire's reins. The cold winter wind tugged at her bonnet, but that was the least of her annoyances. She'd come out here this morning to catch a break from the house, especially from Mr. Baker.

She had nearly forgotten her conversation with Lady Shakerley and Lady Chapman of last week and had been quite surprised when Mr. Baker had shown up. Then came the never-ending addresses. Overwhelming wasn't a strong enough word. She was drowning in all the attention he was determined to heap upon her. Though she still stood by her original design to give Mr. Baker every benefit and truly get to know him, this morning she'd needed a break.

All she'd received for her trouble was a branch across the face.

"May I help you dismount, miss?" a stablehand said from several paces away.

She was tempted to tell him no and simply leap from the saddle if only to prove to herself that she still had some modicum of control in her own life. But such would be foolish. She'd probably twist her ankle or even break her neck. Then, she wouldn't be able to slip out of *any* room Mr. Baker happened to walk in to.

"Yes, if you don't mind," she said.

The young man brought over a mounting block and gently handed her down.

"I hope you enjoyed your ride, miss."

"I did," she lied. "Thank you."

Once she had both feet on the ground, the stablehand bowed briefly, picked up the mounting block, and shot her a smile before turning away.

He paused in his turn, his gaze centering on her left cheek, and his brow dropped.

Oh, drat; she had been worried her encounter with the low hanging branch had left its mark. Oh, well; she'd endured her reputation being left in tatters; having everyone at Hedgewood Manor see her with an unbecoming red line across her face didn't seem too bad.

"It is only a little scratch," she said, hoping to wave off his concern.

"It don't look like a little scratch to me. Beggin' yer pardon, miss." He added the last bit with a bow.

"It doesn't hurt, truly," she said. Which was mostly, if not completely, true.

"Do you want me to send for the doctor? He's mighty good."

"Gracious, no. It's not as bad as all that."

He bowed one more time and began leading Starfire back toward the stables.

Alone once again, Helena tugged on her gloves and righted her riding habit. Hedgewood Maze loomed up before her, reminding her that she had better go back inside. She would be missed soon if she didn't. Who knew what would happen then?

Unfortunately, it would probably be something close to Mr. Baker seeking her out, or Lord Chapman refusing to meet her gaze. What had changed in him? They'd become such good friends, and then, almost overnight, he'd stopped speaking to her. She'd tried several times to broach this topic or that with him, but inevitably, he made his excuses and left. The warmth and comfort she'd always found in his company had shriveled up, too. Instead, she was in a constant state of unease. Not even her well-practiced optimism could chase away her maudlin mood.

Helena pulled in a deep breath. The cold air filled her lungs, taking residence inside her. She closed her eyes for a minute and soaked in the sun's rays. She'd hoped that getting out of doors and riding on horseback would work its usual magic. But, after a minute, the cold came back, pecking away at her hands and toes. She'd dressed warmly for her ride, but it was bitterly cold and, today, she felt it.

Shaking her head, Helena turned her sights on Hedgewood Manor and walked inside. At least it was warm there. And, just perhaps, if she were careful, she might make it to her bedchamber without being waylaid by a certain aging man who only ever referred to her as something he could eat. It had been 'sweetmeat' last night, then 'my plum pudding' that morning at breakfast. Even as she was trying to get away, he'd called her his 'apple dumpling.'

Christina came around a corner just as Helena was passing by.

"There you are!" Christina hurried over, a stack of papers in her hand. "You'll never imagine what Eleanor and I found only this morning."

Helena glanced about the corridor, but Mr. Baker was nowhere to be seen. With any luck, he wouldn't catch her standing here with his niece.

"It's music for the harp." Christina held out several sheets. "I'm dying to hear it played. Do you think you could manage?"

The score promised to be lovely. But did she dare? Helena's gaze darted about the corridor.

"My uncle has gone into Dunwell with my cousin. I believe Lord Forbes, Mother, and Mrs. Andrews accompanied them."

Helena gave Christina a thankful smile. "Then yes, let me change quickly, and I'll meet you in the music room."

"Excellent." Christina giggled and moved away.

Feeling lighter than she had all morning, Helena hurried to her room and rushed her abigail through changing out of her warm riding habit and into a more comfortable morning dress. Moreover, since she was feeling a touch better at the thought of playing her music, she decided to scribble off another short letter to her Uncle Scrooge. Another insistent invitation to Christmas Day dinner seemed in order. He may have been rude and dismissive, but he was her only family, and she wasn't giving up on him just yet.

"A little powder for your cheek, ma'am?" her abigail asked after Helena had folded and sealed the quickly written letter.

"I had not planned on it," she said, placing a hand against her cheek. It burned slightly at the touch and she pulled her hand away. "Lady Christina did not think anything amiss."

Her abigail watched her silently, clearly knowing it wasn't proper to disagree but not wanting to agree with her either.

Helena turned toward the mirror and inspected her face. A long, bright red line crossed her left cheek. A few drops of dried blood sat darkly near her temple.

"Now that I think about it, I believe Lady Christina only saw the right side of my face." They hadn't been conversing long, and Christina had been rather taken in with the music she was holding. Helena lifted a rag and began scrubbing at the dried blood. "Yes, I think a little might be called for."

Once the scratch was cleaned and powdered over, it wasn't nearly as noticeable. Still, Helena's abigail pulled her hair to the left side, allowing it to cascade over her shoulder, covering most of the deepest part of the scratch. Her abigail then took the letter for Uncle Scrooge and left to see it franked.

Finally feeling presentable and thrilled for another chance to play the harp, Helena hurried down the stairs and toward the music room.

Music came from down the hall, but Fredrick was fairly certain it wasn't a harp he was hearing. Pity that. Or perhaps it was just as well.

These days, he could hardly tell up from down, let alone what he wished or didn't wish to hear. Still, his feet carried him down the corridor in the general direction of the music room. After all, if some of the ladies were playing, there was a greater chance that Helena would be present as well. Though he was still determined to avoid her as much as possible, he didn't want to miss out on hearing her play.

He turned the corner and pulled to a stop. Helena stood in the corridor before him, facing the music room door. She didn't seem to have noticed him but remained motionless where she stood.

Should he announce himself? He *was* trying to avoid her. Silently, Fredrick took a step backward. If he could just round the corner before she turned and saw him, before she turned and *smiled* at him—

Except, she wasn't smiling. Not in the least. He froze, studying her closely. Though he could only see her profile, her jaw was taut, and her lips were pursed in a most unhappy manner. Whatever could be so wrong? Fredrick strode down the corridor toward her.

Voices from inside the music room slipped out the closed door. Though someone continued to play the pianoforte—he thought he recognized the song as one Christina had been practicing lately—there were clearly two other women inside conversing as well.

"Frankly, I think it a blessing *someone* is taking such interest in Miss Spencer."

Fredrick would know that condescending tone anywhere: Miss Wynn. The second woman gave a reply, one too soft for Fredrick to make out.

"I don't." Miss Wynn spoke over whomever else was in the room with her. "I know it's Christian to speak as though that little mess up with Lord Chapman is all in the past. Certainly, I pretend as much whenever she is around. But we are grown, and facts must be faced. This holiday house party only illustrates that most gentlemen see her as unfit for proper society."

"How do you figure?" Fredrick still couldn't place the other woman's voice.

"Why, if not for her reputation, *someone* would surely have offered for her by now."

Her reputation? What utter rot. Reaching Helena, Fredrick placed a hand against her arm.

She pulled away, her brow set low.

He hadn't expected that. She'd seemed quite willing, *wanting* even, to find comfort in him at the ball. Why, then, was she pulling back now?

"I thought you were avoiding me," she whispered softly enough that no one in the music room would hear.

Yes, he had been. Only, how did he explain why? *I realized I was in love with you about the same time Baker showed up,* at your request, *as a solution to all your problems. A bit awkward, I must say.*

"So," the other woman's tone was sharp and traveled to them easily, "if a woman is not offered for within four weeks of meeting a man, he sees her as beneath him? What, then, does that say about *you*, Miss Wynn?"

Bravo. It wasn't Christina or Eleanor standing up for

Helena. It must be Lady Emma. She rose quite a bit in his estimation at hearing her defend her friend.

Helena's gaze left him and moved toward the music room doors. "She's right, you know."

"Of course your friend is right. Just because—"

"No." The word was firm. With her auburn hair cascading down the side of her face, Fredrick was struck again by how much he wanted to be near her and never have to part. "Miss Wynn. We've all been fooling ourselves, thinking I could make a match." She shook her head. "Miss Wynn is correct. My tarnished reputation is far too much for most gentlemen to overlook, especially since I have no large dowry to tempt them with."

It wouldn't matter to him if she had no dowry at all; he'd always find her plenty tempting. "Miss Wynn is simply jealous." He moved up closer to her once more. "She is not nearly so witty nor enjoyable to be around"—he lifted his hand, aching to cup her cheek as he had the night of the holiday ball—"and she knows—"

She winced at his touch and Fredrick pulled his hand away. An angry red line cut down her cheek from just below her forehead toward her jaw. A protective heat surged through him.

"What the blazes happened?" His gaze moved to his own glove, which had come away with a bit of powder on it. The cut was probably even deeper than it appeared.

"Apparently, Starfire was not in the mood for a ride this morning," she said. "He kept trying to unseat me by riding close to trees with low branches."

"Idiot horse," Fredrick muttered. He pushed her hair out of the way and inspected the cut further. He understood now why her hair had been left hanging over her shoulder. It covered the worst part of the cut which was higher on her face. "I don't think it will need stitches."

"Starfire will be disappointed to hear that."

Fredrick's gaze dropped to hers. There were tears lining the bottom of her lashes, yet she smiled in spite of them. Someday he would really have to ask her how she managed to do that.

His thumb, almost of its own accord, stroked her cheek, below the cut where it would not irritate. "I have half a mind to march out there and unseat Starfire. See how he likes it."

She laughed softly. "You'd have to let him ride you first, and then the neighborhood doctor would certainly be needed."

Her gaze met his. Her green eyes seemed to search his own, looking for something. Was it reassurance? Or simply hope that she needed? Then her brow dropped, and she pulled away again.

What had happened?

Whatever it was, he didn't like it. Not in the least.

The music room door opened, and he became suddenly aware his hand was still midair, left there when Helena had pulled away. He dropped it quickly and took a small step back. As he suspected, Lady Emma moved out of the room. She took one look at Helena and opened her arms.

"How much of that did you hear?" she asked, wrapping Helena in a hug.

"Enough." Helena took a shuddering breath and pulled away from Lady Emma. "Please don't lie to me and say she's wrong. I know she speaks the truth."

Fredrick looked to Lady Emma—surely he could depend on *her* to help him talk sense into Helena.

Instead, however, Lady Emma only shrugged. "But on the bright side, you *do* seem to have Mr. Baker's full attention."

That was the bright side? Fredrick nearly groaned aloud in frustration.

"At least I don't have to worry he'll consider me bitter. I've always wanted to be known as having a sweet disposition."

Lady Emma laughed at Helena's painful joke, but even she couldn't get it to sound authentic. "Moreover," she hurried on, clearly trying to cover for her lack of sincere amusement at Helena's situation, "we have a witness right here who can testify that Mr. Baker will treat you well. Is that not so, Lord Chapman?"

The tightness around Lady Emma's last few words made it clear she was not *asking* him to speak fondly of his uncle, but rather demanding he did.

But, oh, the look in Helena's eyes. She needed comforting now more than any other time he'd ever known her. It was possible to lie and say his uncle was a fraud and worse, but he couldn't. Because, truth was, his uncle, while a little silly at times, was an upstanding man.

"I have never known him to be unkind to anyone," he answered honestly. "Be they gentleman, lady, or servant. Baker has always proved himself considerate and thoughtful." Sometimes to a fault, like the time he had tried to arrange Fredrick and Helena's marriage without their knowledge.

What a fool Fredrick had been not to simply go along with the whole thing. To think, he and Helena could have been husband and wife by now.

Helena's lips tipped up on one side. The smile wasn't exactly forced, but neither was it vibrant. "Thank you both. Now, if you'll excuse me, I think I'll go lie down before dinner. I have some things to think through—and to come to terms with."

With another half-smile, she walked away. Fredrick wished he could go with her. Walk with her, wrap his arm around her shoulders and pull her close once more.

"What of that did *you* hear?" Lady Emma asked.

"Enough to confirm my suspicions that Miss Wynn is a determined gossip." And not one he cared to ever share a Christmas with again.

"So," Lady Emma drew the word out, "you heard what she said about you?"

Him? Lord Chapman's gaze snapped back to Lady Emma. "No." Dare he ask?

Lady Emma's gaze turned hard. "She claimed your mother brought Baker here for you."

"For me?" That made no sense. "How does she figure?"

Lady Emma glanced back toward the music room, then motioned down the corridor, the opposite direction Helena had fled. He still wanted to go after Helena, but he felt she was sincere in her desire to be alone just now. Moreover, if Lady Emma could enlighten him as to why Helena was suddenly pulling away, he needed to know.

He fell into step beside Lady Emma and after a few paces, she started speaking once more.

"Miss Wynn intimated that the attentions you've paid Helena have all been because you felt guilty over last summer. That you were simply trying to make amends. But being Helena's friend has become too much of a strain, and so Baker has been brought in to save you."

Of all the nasty, mean-hearted things . . .

"It's rubbish. Complete rubbish." Helena would know as much. She of all people would see through Miss Wynn's idle tongue.

"Is it?" Lady Emma pulled to a stop and faced him fully. "The only reason you first spoke to Helena is because we guilted you into it."

Well, that was true. He'd been intent on ignoring her up until that night in the orangery.

"Your attentions since have been largely focused on finding her a husband."

That had not been his idea but was still true.

"Now that Mr. Baker has arrived, you've all but acted as though Helena doesn't even exist."

That point caused a sharp twinge to tighten across his

stomach. Lord Chapman opened his mouth to argue back. "That doesn't mean—"

"She's confused, beaten on all sides. Between the gossip she overhears constantly and the uncertainty of her future, is it any wonder she doesn't know what to believe right now?" Spinning on her heel, Lady Emma stalked off, leaving Fredrick standing in the middle of the corridor alone and feeling quite like a mule.

CHAPTER TWENTY-ONE

"Tell me, Miss Spencer, how have you enjoyed the house party thus far?" Lord Forbes asked.

Oh, dear, how did one answer a question like that? With her hand on his arm, Helena glanced about the back lawn, using the time to gather her thoughts. There was the malicious gossip which she'd hoped to prove herself above but hadn't. There was Fredrick whom she'd grown close to, only to have him suddenly turn away. There was Mr. Baker in whom she was determined to see the best yet couldn't find in herself a willingness to accept. There was Uncle Scrooge who still refused to consider her as family.

But one could not say any of that in polite conversation. "It has been most enjoyable," she said. It wasn't exactly a lie; she *had* enjoyed a lot of things this Christmas. Times with Emma, Christina, and Eleanor. The ball a couple of weeks ago. Fredrick.

"I am pleased to hear it. I must confess, I was uncertain when I first arrived and found the gathering so small. But I have found the company pleasing."

His statement was nearly as superficial as her own. What

were the chances he was hiding as much in his socially polite statement as she had been in hers? She'd probably never know.

"I am happy to hear it," Helena replied. Their conversation slipped into an easy silence as they passed the snow-covered roses and continued across the path. If Lord Forbes *had* been hiding troubles in his polite statement, what kind of troubles would they be? The line of thought was irrational at best, foolish at worse. But it was more agreeable than mulling over her own issues yet again.

Suppose Lord Forbes had had the grave misfortune of falling in love this Christmas? She glanced at him out of the corner of her eye. It certainly could not have been with anyone at the house party. He never paid any of the ladies any special attention. A lady in Dunwell, perhaps? Perhaps someone his family would never approve of?

The notion was completely imagined, but it did bring a mischievous smile to her face. Even now, as they walked, she fancied him thinking of his doomed love, wishing she were on his arm instead of Helena.

Since Helena's father had passed and she'd nearly become engaged to Fredrick, only to be branded as tainted when he had refused, she'd set aside thoughts of marrying for love. And yet . . .

What would it be like to walk with someone who made her heart flutter? Or whose touch heated her skin?

Fredrick had, at one point.

She tamped down that train of thought immediately. His actions as of late had made it clear that he only wished for friendship with her. Yes, he was willing to comfort, even hold her, when she was upset. But that didn't mean he cared more for her than he did for his sisters.

The realization was demoralizing in the extreme.

They took a small turn in the garden path and the hedge maze loomed up on their left. Walking above it, Helena was sorely tempted to stop and study the maze, memorize the easiest way in and out. Perhaps then the nightmares would cease. Last night she'd had another one. She'd been awake since well before dawn, having not been able to sleep afterward.

"Are you disappointed you were unable to join us in the maze a few weeks ago?" Lord Forbes asked.

Helena pulled her gaze away from the maze and over to the man beside her.

"Not particularly," she replied. "I find I prefer to be able to see where I am."

Lord Forbes nodded, his flat expression unchanging. "Then I am sure you would love the white cliffs of Dover."

"I do, indeed."

"You have been there?"

"More than once. My father enjoyed seeing all of England, and though I didn't travel with him every time, I did once in a while."

"Dover in early summer," Fredrick said as he walked over, with Miss Wynn on his arm, "is an adventure not to be missed."

So he was talking to her again? "No, it is not," Helena said, turning away and ending the conversation. She shouldn't be mad at Fredrick, not after he'd helped her so much this Christmas. But she was. Some friend he proved to be, deserting her the moment his uncle had shown up to take her off his hands.

Lord Forbes asked Miss Wynn if she'd ever been to Dover, and as they spoke, Helena kept her gaze turned away, willing her mind to wander back to happier days gone by. Standing atop the white cliffs with her father, the breeze off the sea blowing her hair out of its pins; savoring fresh fish at every dinner; lazily strolling arm in arm with him . . . that was her favorite memory of all.

An excited cry drew everyone's attention to where Lord Ellis, astride a large black horse, came riding up.

"Lord Forbes, Miss Wynn, Lord Chapman," he said, even while dismounting. "I have found the most enormous fallen tree; it would make an excellent yule log."

Helena did not miss that she'd been excluded from the list of people Lord Ellis wished to speak to. Since their encounter in the stables, he'd ignored her more and more, save the one dance at the Adley's ball. He must have been pressured into asking her then. It was a bit of a silver lining from that dreadful day. Still, she did wish to be done with always being excluded. She wished to be considered on equal footing with her acquaintances, as she'd once been. Would marrying Mr. Baker provide that for her? As the wife of a respected gentleman, it very well might.

Lord Forbes, for his part, did not seem to have noticed Lord Ellis's lack of inclusion. The smug look on Miss Wynn's face clearly showed she *had*, however. But how came she to be walking with Fredrick? Helena knew he did not care for her company. Then again, Miss Wynn was not easily swayed once an idea entered her head.

Fredrick, however, wasn't appearing to pay attention to Lord Ellis, or any of them. He was looking down at the maze and scowling. Helena followed his gaze. Christina and Topper were walking, arm in arm, toward the entrance. That explained the scowl. With all that had happened as of late, and with how little she saw Fredrick, Helena hadn't had the opportunity to tell him of hers and Christina's conversation regarding Topper. Helena pulled her lips to the side; she needed to tell him and soon.

When Miss Wynn expressed the desire to walk over and speak with Lord Ellis, Fredrick declined. Lord Forbes readily offered to walk with her, extending the arm that Helena was not holding on to.

"You go ahead," Helena said. "I think I shall enjoy the view from here a bit longer."

She waited until Lord Forbes and Miss Wynn were out of earshot. "I spoke with Christina a few days ago. She admitted to sincerely liking him."

Fredrick's only response was to snort.

"She actually asked for my permission to further their . . . connection."

"Why would she be asking you?"

"Because she, Eleanor, and Emma all agreed to help me find a match. She was only being considerate."

"Well, then I'm sure you're all thrilled my uncle has joined the party."

Helena placed her hands on her hips at the sound of his sarcastic, dry tone. *She* was glad he had joined them? Mr. Baker was an act of desperation—one she only had to consider thanks to Fredrick. But this conversation wasn't about them and she didn't care to make it so. "Fredrick, it is time you stop being such a bulldog. Topper has acted nothing less than honorable toward your sister thus far."

Fredrick slowly shook his head back and forth. "He may only be biding his time, tricking us all into trusting him."

Truly? "Don't you think you're overreacting just a little?"

"Most likely." He ran a hand over the back of his neck. "You are right; he hasn't done anything that . . . now, hold on." Fredrick shook a finger toward his sister and Topper.

Helena turned and looked down at the couple just in time to see them slip into the maze.

"No gentleman would lead a lady into such a secluded place as that when it was only the two of them," Fredrick said, his tone quickly turning sharp. He took hold of Helena's hand and began pulling her toward the downhill path which led to the maze's entrance. "*This* is just the sort of thing I have been expecting."

The maze quickly rose up on Helena's left. In no more than half a dozen steps, she could no longer see the tops of the hedges. "Surely they only mean to go for a short stroll." It was steadily growing too cold to do more than that. "You don't need my help in ascertaining your sister's safety."

He gave her hand a squeeze. "Of course I do. I can't very well go in alone. It'll look like I'm following after them with no other intention than to spy."

"That *is* your only intention," Helena said, dryly.

"Didn't you ever hear that appearances are everything? With us walking *together*, it will *look* like we, too, are simply taking a stroll."

"Only worried about propriety when it concerns your sister, hmm?" Helena asked, even as panic built in her chest.

The hedges were ever so tall now. Was it just her, or was it much colder here than nearer the house? "Everyone will be heading back indoors soon. Why not wait for them until then?"

He pulled her through the towering entrance. "You clearly have never been a brother before."

Helena's heart beat so loudly, she could hear it pulsing. "Clearly." It was all she could manage to say.

Which was utter foolishness. There was no reason for her to be nervous or shaking. She was walking through a perfectly respectable hedge maze—not at all like the one in her nightmares. There were no incorporeal spirits casting long dark shadows. The path was well cared for, and not a blade of grass cut at her ankles or pulled at her skirts.

Fredrick continued speaking. Helena tried to listen, but she was needing most of her attention to keep her breathing steady. This would only be a short walk. Surely they would find Christina and Topper soon. Then it would only be a quick turn around, and they'd be out within minutes.

A twig snapped somewhere behind them. Helena spun around, but the path was empty.

"Come, I think they must have gone this way." Fredrick pulled her further into the maze.

She could always tell him she didn't wish to continue—but what excuse would she give? That she was childish? That she was scared because of a bad dream? No, she was far too mature to fall to pieces over—

"You take that path, and I'll take this one," Fredrick said.

"What? We're splitting up?" Helena could hear the panic in her own voice. If she didn't take control of her emotions immediately, she wouldn't have to explain to Fredrick that she was a bit of an imbecile. He'd figure it all out on his own.

"Don't go far," he said, already letting go of her and walking away. "Just check around either corner and come right back here."

He strode off without looking back.

Helena glanced around her. The sun was setting and only tinges of pink and orange could be seen above a few of the hedges. They needed to find Christina and Topper and leave as soon as possible, otherwise, they risked being caught out in the dark. A chill ran down her spine at the thought.

Helena hurried forward. She could do this. She could ignore her tight stomach and racing heart. She would stay focused. Find Christina. Locate Topper.

And, later, she'd corner Fredrick and ring a peal over his head for dragging her in here.

Fredrick turned a corner. They couldn't have gotten far. He and Helena were only a few minutes behind Christina and Topper. Then again, if he'd taken a wrong turn near the entrance, it might be quite a while still before he found them. Blasted maze.

If Topper so much as gave him a single reason to think he might have less than honorable intentions—

Soft voices made him slow his step. It certainly sounded like Christina speaking, but he wasn't close enough to tell for sure, let alone make out any of the words. Fredrick tread carefully; he'd wanted to make sure his sister was safe but wasn't eager to announce his presence.

The voices grew even quieter. Was he moving the wrong direction? He could have sworn they'd been coming from just up ahead. The path Fredrick was on came to a *T*. He poked his head out slowly. Nothing to the left. He swung to the right.

Topper and Christina stood only a few paces away, facing one another. Fredrick slipped up close to the hedge, careful to stay hidden. Christina would kill him if she ever found out he was spying on her, but he couldn't, in good conscience, walk away. This was the best compromise he could come up with. If she ever did find out, she'd just have to come to understand as much.

"I got you something," Topper said. He reached into a pocket and pulled out a small, rectangular box.

A gift? That was rather forward. One black mark against Topper.

Christina took hold of it, her smile radiant, and pulled open the lid. "Oh, it's lovely!"

Topper reached inside the box, drawing out a long chain with something small dangling from the center. Moving around behind Christina, he secured the necklace about her neck.

Christina pressed the charm closer to her with a gloved hand. "I love it."

Fredrick opened and closed a fist—he wished he could fidget, but doing so would risk making too much noise. Watching something that was clearly meant to be private was quickly becoming most uncomfortable for him. Part of him felt he truly ought to move away, while another part of him protested, saying this was just the sort of thing a cad would do before forcing himself on an unsuspecting woman.

Neither part was strong enough to overwhelm the other, and Fredrick found himself rooted to the spot.

Topper placed his hands on Christina's shoulders and whispered something too low for Fredrick to hear. Whatever it was, it put Christina to the blush—another black mark—but it also made her smile, so he had not said anything that had caused his sister alarm.

Topper moved back around and faced Christina once more. Perhaps it was just as well Fredrick should make his presence known now. He'd given the gift; there was nothing more for Topper to do—nothing honorable, anyway.

Fredrick lifted a foot, ready to step out and appear all nonchalant, as though he'd only accidentally come across them.

"Do you truly like it?" Topper asked.

Christina placed a hand against the necklace and nodded.

"Good, because it's actually half of a matched set." Topper took hold of Christina's hand and dropped to one knee, pulling out a golden ring.

Fredrick pulled back once more.

"Christina, my sweet," Topper spoke loud enough for Fredrick to hear this time, "I came here only in the hopes of finding a bit of holiday cheer, a bit of enjoyment. But instead, I found something far better. I found you. Never have I known such beauty or such kindness. Please, I cannot leave without knowing you share my love. Please say you'll marry me."

"Yes," Christina said enthusiastically. "Yes, with all my heart."

Topper stood and pulled Christina close, kissing her.

Fredrick stepped away from the corner. Never had he heard a more sincere statement than the one Topper had just uttered. Helena had been right all along. Topper *had* been honorable in his attentions. The crunch of footfalls alerted him that Topper and Christina were walking his way. Fredrick ducked down a side path and allowed them to pass him. They walked by, her arms wrapped around his, large smiles on both their faces and eyes which only saw one another.

What a bumbling, overprotective fool he'd been. At least his vigilance hadn't caused any harm or embarrassment. Being careful to remain unseen, Fredrick followed them through the maze and back toward the entrance. Although, once he told everything to Helena, he very well might become the brunt of more than one joke.

HELENA REACHED A TURNOFF. SHE TOOK A FEW STEPS DOWN the path to the right, but she could neither see nor hear anyone in that direction. Turning around, she searched a different path off the other way. Still no luck. She closed her eyes momentarily, even as her breathing sped up.

Gracious, but the high hedge walls felt ever so much more intimidating when alone. Fredrick was certainly going to hear from her about this. Let him follow her anywhere he so chose, but next time she wasn't going to be party to it.

Helena paused in the middle of the path. This wasn't Fredrick's fault. She'd willingly followed him in here. Christina was her friend, too, and she also wished to ascertain that Christina was safe.

Moreover, this was nothing but a hedge maze. Anyone with sense would simply keep their wits about them and find their way out. They wouldn't shake or tremble. But she was. She took hold of her skirt and hurried forward, willing her breathing to remain calm.

Helena stepped down another path but still could not find anyone. Rubbing her hands over either arm, she turned and hurried back toward where Fredrick had unceremoniously abandoned her.

Only, he wasn't there. An early night wind rustled the topmost leaves of the hedges around her, wailing high above her head. The chill of the wind was blocked by the walls around her, but she could still feel the temperature dropping. A harsh shiver shook her. Where was Fredrick?

Her skin crawled and she rubbed furiously at her arms. There were no spooks here. No spooks. No spooks.

Helena turned slowly around—but, wait. This wasn't the same spot he'd left her. Helena went cold. She hurried down the path she'd just come. But nothing here looked familiar. Or it did—it all looked the same. Blast. Helena wrapped her arms tightly against her stomach but couldn't stop shaking.

The last rays of the sun were quickly disappearing. Her throat felt as though it was closing off. She wasn't safe here. She couldn't stay. She rushed down one path and then around a corner. This path looked exactly like the one behind her. Just like the one before that, too. No matter how many paths she took, she couldn't find her way back to where Fredrick had left her. She couldn't find the entrance.

There was no way out.

As she groped her away around the maze, the sky overhead turned orange, then pink, then purple, and finally a dark black. Helena couldn't stop shivering. Her teeth chattered so loudly, they seemed to pound against her head.

It was as though no matter how many turns she made, how many paths she took, she always ended up exactly where she started. It was just like her nightmare. In complete darkness, she urged her feet to continue walking.

Her foot snagged on something and she stumbled forward, her right shoulder colliding into the hedge. Sticks and twigs pricked and scraped against her, sending shots of immobilizing pain across her whole form.

Helena struggled to breathe against the ache as she dropped to one knee. She couldn't breathe. She lifted a hand to her throat but found nothing there. Still, no matter how much she tried, she couldn't seem to draw in enough air.

She couldn't feel her feet, and her hands moved as though awkward clubs.

But she couldn't stay.

She wasn't safe.

She had to keep trying to get up . . . had to escape.

CHAPTER TWENTY-TWO

As they reached the entrance to the maze, Topper slowed his step and turned toward Christina. "Let me go see if I can find your brother." He kissed her forehead. "We'll talk more tonight."

Christina nodded her agreement. They walked out of the maze, Topper turning one way and Christina another. Fredrick held back a bit. With Topper looking for him now, he needed to be doubly sure he wasn't spotted leaving the maze.

And where was Helena? He'd felt certain he would have caught sight of her as he made his way out. Christina and Topper had been most helpful, though unknowingly so, and walked directly by the spot where he and Helena had split. She hadn't been there. Had she already given up on finding Christina and left? She had seemed rather put out at him for dragging her into the maze. All the more so because she'd already been upset with him.

Fredrick peeked out from the hedge maze. No one was looking toward the entrance. He quickly stepped out and hurried after Christina, putting as much distance between himself and the entrance as possible.

His sister joined a group of women. Just past Christina, Fredrick caught sight of a dark blue pelisse. So Helena had come out of the maze already. His steps slowed. He ached to walk up to her and tell her all he'd seen. But it wouldn't be wise.

A footman walked up to Fredrick. "Pardon me, sir, but Lady Chapman has requested everyone return to the house. Dinner is about to be served."

Fredrick glanced toward the sky. The sun's rays were all but gone. Soon it would be dark. "Yes, of course." They'd stayed outside far longer than any of them had originally planned.

The footman moved on to inform the other guests. Alone, Fredrick slowly made his way back toward the house. No doubt, Topper would be wanting to speak with him, possibly even before they all sat down to dinner. Wouldn't Helena crow over his head when she learned how right she had been?

Fredrick reached the house before the women did. Standing just inside the back parlor doors, he watched their approach. With their heads bent close to one another, they seemed far too occupied to walk quickly at all.

"Excuse me, Lord Chapman."

Topper had found him at last. "Yes?"

"I wondered if I might have a word with you."

He could string the man along or just give in immediately. One sounded far more fun, the other far safer, assuming Topper would most likely repeat their conversation to Christina after the matter was settled.

"It is a matter of some delicacy."

The women drew nearer, and the one wearing the dark blue turned her face toward him. It wasn't Helena. Instead, it was Lady Andrews. And now that Fredrick looked closer, he couldn't imagine why he'd thought her to be Helena in the first place. The cut of the pelisse was different, and the woman's height was wrong.

"Perhaps," Topper continued in his silence, "we might remove to—"

Fredrick put a hand on his shoulder stopping him. "Have you seen Helena?"

Topper's mouth shut with a snap. Then his brow creased. "I saw Miss Spencer earlier today, but I can't say I've seen her lately."

Blast. Fredrick flung the door open and hurried back out toward the group of women walking his way.

"Where is Helena?" he asked the group at large.

The women glanced about at each other and shook their heads. A few said things like, "I thought she returned to the house already," or "I haven't seen her."

Fredrick pushed past them. The night was upon them. The clear sky stretched out over the top of the hedge maze. She had to still be in there. Hang him. Spinning, he turned back toward the house. Topper watched him from the doorway.

"Helena is lost in the maze."

Miss Wynn let out a tsk. "I am sure she will return to the house soon. It isn't even snowing tonight."

"No," Lord Forbes said, his voice as flat as ever. "It's worse. The sky is clear."

Lord Forbes was correct. A clear sky was far more dangerous than a cloudy one, for at least clouds kept the temperature from dropping too low. On a winter night when the sky was clear, all living things were in danger of freezing.

"Gather the men," Fredrick said.

Topper jumped into action, but Fredrick didn't hang around waiting to see who was willing to join the search. He turned and hurried toward the maze.

"Helena!" Fredrick called for the dozenth time. Hang him and his own irrationality. He should not have followed Christina and Topper in here. Even more so, he should *not* have left Miss Spencer.

This was why he should never have become an earl. This was why his father never should have died and left such responsibilities to him. He'd only been trying his best to watch over his sister, and now he'd placed Helena in very real danger. The night was deucedly cold. A person could die unsheltered on a night like this. He couldn't feel his feet, and he was wearing thick boots. What must Helena's feet feel like by now?

He called again but still heard no answer. How big was this cursed maze? Somewhere, far off, he heard another man call for her. He'd crossed paths with Lord Forbes once and Mr. Andrews twice. No one had seen a trace of Helena. He hadn't heard any other voices besides his own for far too long.

Curse him for dragging her in here.

He had to find her.

"Helena!" he called out again, feeling as much as seeing his way down the path and around a corner. "Helena!"

He took two steps, then paused. In the moonlight, he could barely make out a small form huddled near the base of the hedge.

"Helena?"

The lump on the ground moaned and shifted about slightly. Fredrick hurried forward and dropped to his knees. The pebbles of the path bit hard. Why did everything hurt so much more when one was freezing?

He reached out, his hand resting against her shoulder. It was Helena, all right.

She stirred but didn't open her eyes. He couldn't see her well enough to assess her by the color of her skin or lips. But if he had to guess, he would assume they were both far too blue.

He gave her a gentle shake. "Helena. You have to get up. We have to get you out of here."

She squirmed slightly and let out another groan, her eyes still not opening.

"Come on," Fredrick said, slipping an arm beneath her and lifting her into a sitting position. She was lethargic and wholly unresponsive.

She didn't lift her head; instead, it swung back and forth. He needed to get her warm. Keeping one arm around her, else he was certain she'd collapse, he shrugged one arm out of his greatcoat. Switching her to his other arm, he shrugged the rest of the way out. Lud, but it was frigid. Fredrick draped the coat about her shoulders and tucked her close to his side.

Fredrick shifted about and lifted her into his arms. The way she sagged was worrisome. Was she conscious at all?

"Can you wake up?" he said as he moved back the way he'd come. "You need to wake up, Helena."

Her face scrunched up, but she did nothing more.

He jostled her slightly. "Come on, it's not safe to sleep right now."

"Fredrick?"

Oh, thank goodness. "Yes, my love. I need you to wake up, all right?"

"I was so scared."

Being stranded in a maze as dark was falling would be enough to scare anyone. "You're safe now. I've got you."

"It was just like my nightmare."

He glanced back down at her. He hadn't been aware she struggled with nightmares. "What was just like your nightmare?" He needed her to keep talking to be sure she didn't go back to sleep.

"The hedge maze." Her words slurred a bit, and she still hadn't opened her eyes. But at least she was somewhat lucid.

"And I went and dragged you in here, regardless."

Her hand slipped out from beneath his greatcoat, and she patted him on the chest. "You didn't know."

She needed to keep herself inside the coat, but with both his arms occupied in carrying her, he couldn't put it back himself. "It seems all I ever do around you is apologize."

"You care . . ." Her hand grew heavier against him, and her words jumbled. "That's nothing to apologize . . ."

"Helena?" He shifted her about in his arms again. "Helena, keep talking to me. You have to stay awake, remember?" He'd never forgive himself if she wasn't all right. But no matter what he did, Helena didn't wake back up.

He needed to get her warm. Surely they were almost out of this cursed maze. A few strides later, Topper came into view. Fredrick instructed the man to hurry ahead to let the house know Helena had been found but was gravely cold.

Topper ran off. He must have met up with some of the other men, however, for soon a great cry started as first one and then another man shouted that Miss Spencer had been found.

Fredrick made the trek back to the house as quickly as he could. Stepping into the candlelight of the back parlor, Fredrick's fears were confirmed. Helena's skin was ghostly white and her lips a strange, unnatural blue.

FREDRICK PACED DOWN THE HALLWAY, TURNED, AND WALKED back, passing Baker pacing the other way. Doctor Lock had come and gone some time ago. He hadn't had much to say, but he had relayed that Helena had woken up and spoken to him, she was slowly regaining her normal color, and he would be back to check on her again the next day.

With another turn, he moved by her bedchamber door, not bothering to look at Baker this time. Lady Emma, Lady Shakerley, Lady Andrews, and his own mother were in with Helena right now. But they had, understandably, refused to allow any of the gentlemen into the room. Understandable, but frustrating.

"She'll be all right," Baker said, pausing across the hallway from her door.

Fredrick shook his head. This was all his fault, and he wouldn't be eased into false hope.

His silence didn't stop Baker from speaking on, however. "I've grown more fond of that girl than even I expected to," he said. "She's sharp, optimistic, and strong."

If he was trying to make Fredrick feel better, he was doing a lousy job of it.

"You need to know." Baker's voice turned firm. "We all have grown fond of her. Your mother, your sisters. We just want to see her happy."

Something inside Fredrick twisted painfully. He stopped his pacing and faced Baker fully. "Are you saying you two have an understanding?" He hadn't thought things had progressed so fast as all that.

"I'm saying if she will have me, I plan to give Miss Spencer the best sort of life possible."

Fredrick didn't have time to think through what he was hearing before the bedchamber door opened, and his mother stepped out.

"She is awake."

"How is she?" Baker asked.

At the same time, Fredrick asked, "Can I speak with her?"

Lady Chapman glanced between them. "She's asked to speak with Mr. Baker."

What? Fredrick stood there, shocked into silence, as his uncle moved into the room.

His mother remained out in the hallway, the door shutting behind her.

Even with the door shut, Fredrick could hear Baker's low voice. Someone answered him. Helena, perhaps? He couldn't believe she was up and speaking and wasn't willing to see him.

"Is she truly all right?" he asked his mother.

"Yes. She will make a full recovery."

"And there won't be any long term . . . problems?"

The corner of Lady Chapman's mouth twitched up. "We checked each of her fingers and toes. She is going to be just fine."

Thank the heavens. His gaze returned to the door just behind his mother. Had she been upset he'd insisted she go into the maze? Of course, before that, she'd clearly been hurt at his avoidance of her. And well before that, there had been last summer. But between last summer and Baker showing up, there had been so many moments—intimate, undeniable moments.

"Perhaps," Lady Chapman said, "if you come back tomorrow afternoon, she'll be more up to seeing you."

"Is that what Father would have done?" he asked.

Lady Chapman's eyes turned sad. "I couldn't say. He never dragged me into a maze and left me there." With that nonc-too-gentle remark, she slipped back into the room and shut the door firmly.

CHAPTER TWENTY-THREE

Fredrick sat down heavily into the small wooden chair. About him, the pub buzzed and hummed with life. After Helena had refused to speak to him, he'd tried going to bed. But he'd hardly slept. When dawn came, he'd dressed quickly and returned to pacing outside Helena's room. He was informed almost immediately, however, that Helena was sleeping and wasn't to be disturbed.

After that, Fredrick couldn't stand to remain at Hedgewood Manor. Helena didn't need him—didn't want him. And he was going crazy standing about waiting for her to be willing to speak with him. So he'd had a horse saddled and left. He hadn't truly been heading any specific direction, but when he'd come across this pub, stopping for a drink had seemed a good idea.

Now, he wasn't so sure. For such a cold morning, everyone seemed annoyingly cheerful.

"Good mornin' to ye," a man in dirt-covered clothes said as he pulled out a chair and situated himself across from Fredrick. "And a merry Christmas Eve, too."

Fredrick didn't know what to say; he'd rather been hoping

for a few minutes of solitude to better sort through his current predicament. But the man's second statement caught him by surprise every bit as much as his forwardness.

"Is it Christmas Eve already?" he asked.

"Aye," the man said, waving two companions over. "It be, and a right happy one at that."

Gads, he'd completely forgotten what today was. Perhaps he ought to do as Topper had done and buy a present for the woman he loved.

Unasked, the man's two friends sat on either side of the table. Apparently, Fredrick was not to have a quiet morning to himself.

"I'm Martin," the first man said. "These be my jolly companions, Captain Bones"—the man to Fredrick's left, whose clothes marked him as a man from the sea, nodded—"and Thomas." The third man also nodded; though his clothes showed he was from the working class, like Martin, they didn't tell Fredrick his profession.

"You must forgive our intrusion," Thomas said, "but we only get together once a year. Between Martin working the mines, Captain Bones sailing the ocean, and myself seeing to a lighthouse, our time together is short."

If that was so, then Fredrick could not understand why they'd chosen to sit with him instead of finding their own quiet table.

"Still." Captain Bones picked up the narrative—and what kind of name was 'Captain Bones' anyways?—"We always try to find one soul who looks more downcast than we so that we might cheer him up a bit."

"Always makes Christmas feel a little brighter when one has helped another," said Martin.

"The coin you insist on staking on the matter always brings a smile to my face," added Thomas, sotto voce.

"And I'm that gentleman?" Fredrick asked.

The three men nodded in unison.

"Now, is it money or a woman?" Captain Bones asked. "Thomas is a right dab hand with blunt, and Martin knows a thing or two about wives and the like. He's had five of them."

"Five wives?" Fredrick stared at the man in shock.

Martin only laughed. "Not all at once."

What a peculiar three he'd stumbled upon—or had stumbled upon him, as it were. "And where do you come in, Captain Bones?"

The captain's smile turned menacing. "Anytime there's a bloke who needs more of a heavy hand when learning about Christmas generosity, *that's* when I come in."

Good to know.

"All right," Thomas said, leaning across the table, "now that you know us"—that was a stretch in Fredrick's estimation—"spill it. Money or woman?"

"A toff like that don't have a woman," Martin hissed at Thomas. "He'd have a *lady*."

Thomas only lifted his gaze heavenward and shook his head.

Meanwhile, Martin chuckled, "And judging by the toff's face, it *is* a lady."

What was Fredrick to do? There was no point in denying it. He shrugged and agreed with a nod.

"Ha!" Martin crowed, slapping Thomas across the shoulder. "This one's mine." He placed his great arms atop the table and leaned over it. "First off, what did you do to make her angry?"

In for a penny, in for a pound, as they say. "Recently? Or ever?"

Captain Bones whistled low. "Looks like we found a dilly this year."

"It's all very complicated," Fredrick said.

"You best tell it quick then," said Martin.

So Fredrick did. He started with his father passing away, then his uncle's machinations the previous summer and all it had meant for Helena. He told of coming to Hedgewood Manor, completely unaware that she would be there, too. He explained his agreement to help her reestablish herself among society by aiding her search for a husband. Though he didn't go into details regarding their friendship turning into more for him, he believed the three men were smart enough to figure it out.

Lastly, he told of how he had pulled Helena into the maze the night before and unintentionally left her there, only to find her and hear her confess about her nightmares.

Thomas whistled long and low. "You've your work cut out for you on this one, Martin."

Martin, for his part, was watching Fredrick carefully. For a moment, though dressed in the dirtiest clothes Fredrick had ever beheld, and with a frame which proved he'd worked with his hands all his life, he appeared a most thoughtful, wise individual. The look in his expression denoted someone in deep thought, someone a gentleman would be wise to sit up and listen to.

"You care for the lass?" Martin asked.

"Deeply," Fredrick confessed.

"She care for you?"

Fredrick hesitated on that one. "I don't know."

Thomas and Captain Bones exchanged a glance. It could have been a "yup, this one's an idiot" look, or it could have been a "how do we let him down easy?" look. Fredrick wasn't sure. Neither option filled him with very much optimism.

"You plan on bein' good to her?" Thomas asked.

"Of course." And yet, Fredrick shook his head and leaned back. "As good as I know how. Lately, I've started thinking that's not nearly good enough." How did a man live up to all that was expected of him?

"Raised to be a true gentleman," Martin said with a knowing nod.

Thomas shook his head. "Certainly glad I wasn't."

Martin and Captain Bones seemed to be agreeing, wordlessly.

"See," Martin said, "the problem with expectations is you never actually know if you've reached them."

"The goal keeps moving on you," Thomas added.

"Sucks the joy right outta life," Captain Bones said.

"So I should just toss aside all I've been raised to be and what? Turn to smuggling?"

The three men laughed, but it was Captain Bones who spoke next.

"Na, there are enough blokes doing that already. Just don't be so hard on yourself. And, realize, you gotta captain *your* ship *your* way."

Fredrick wasn't so sure it was as simple as all that.

"He means," Martin said, "don't go giving up on your lady."

"She won't even speak to me, remember?" Fredrick asked.

"She will." Martin expressed far more confidence than Fredrick believed the situation warranted. "You stick around long enough, make it clear you aren't goin' nowhere, and she'll speak to you eventually."

Both Thomas and Captain Bones made silent *oohs* and gave their companion small nods as though bowing to his significant wisdom. The sight was somewhat comical, but Fredrick couldn't deny that Martin was starting to make a lot of sense.

"You know," he said, "you might have something there."

"Sure he has," Thomas said, his chair scraping as he pushed to a stand. "He's done this enough times, he oughta."

Both Martin and Captain Bones stood as well and offered Fredrick their best Christmas wishes and farewells. After tossing a few coins to the owner, they slipped outside. Fredrick watched as the door shut. What a strange group of men.

Fredrick downed the rest of his drink. Whoever they were and however their strange Christmas tradition had gotten started, Fredrick was ready to return to Hedgewood Manor and prove to Helena he was as good a man as his father had been. He was ready to step fully into the role of earl and care for a family of his own. And he'd be hanged if he was going to do it without Helena by his side.

CHAPTER TWENTY-FOUR

"Come, my treacle pie, I would dearly like to hear you sing the catch," Baker said, patting Helena's hand. "If you are feeling up to it."

"I believe I am," Helena said, standing and moving closer to the pianoforte. After sleeping away the morning and half the afternoon, she felt remarkably recovered. Moreover, she had been thankful for the opportunity to place a little distance between herself and Mr. Baker. He was a kind man—overly kind, in fact— but today, she was craving a different man's company.

She'd turned him away in a fit of anger last night, brought on by the pain which bit at her fingers and toes most horribly, and she hadn't seen him since.

Miss Wynn sat at the instrument, a smirk across her face. "Treacle pie? How embarrassing," she whispered softly.

Helena had nothing to say to that. She'd all but consigned herself to becoming Mrs. Baker. She'd wondered when she awoke if perhaps Fredrick would be wanting to see her again, but he was gone. Once again, he'd proved content to let his uncle stand by her side, and he had simply left.

Topper began singing, his voice a deep bass. Christina watched him, clearly in love. Helena was both happy to see her friend so but also dismayed. Had Fredrick only ever seen her as a problem that needed to be solved? As a blight on his conscience? Or, perhaps, he merely considered her a good friend?

It was possible her mind was still working through healing from last night, but she was too confused to know what to think.

Lord Forbes picked up the round next, and only a few measures later, Helena began to sing. Their voices did harmonize well. If she were to spend a Christmas among strangers, confused and alone, at least she'd had plenty of music to help her through it. It felt good to focus on the pleasing things happening in her life. As a woman, there would always be so much she couldn't control, but what she chose to focus on was something no one else could take. She would hold to that now.

The song faded to an end, with first Topper ending his part, then Lord Forbes, and lastly Helena. The applause was light, all except for Mr. Baker. He pounded his two great hands together as though he alone was making up for the absence of an entire audience-filled theatre. Feeling pleased, if slightly embarrassed, Helena moved away from the pianoforte.

Mr. Baker stood and met her halfway back to her seat. Lady Chapman sat beside where he'd been only moments ago. Helena had not noticed the woman had joined them. She was smiling up at Helena, her sincere joy prophesying something more was about to happen. Mr. Baker took hold of her hand and looped it around his arm. "Take a turn with me. There's a book in the library I wish to show you."

The look in his eye seemed to say that a book in the library was the last thing Mr. Baker truly wished to discuss. Nonetheless, had not Helena determined that a lasting connection with a gentleman of status was precisely what she needed?

Steeling herself, Helena nodded her consent. Words would have been better than a mute gesture, but, though she was determined to see her end goal achieved, she had not the heart to actually speak.

Silently, she allowed him to walk her out of the room, down the corridor, and up the stairs. They reached the library doors, and Helena drew herself up as she passed into the room. What she needed—not *wanted* but needed—was a man who would save her from a life of poverty and rejection. It wasn't as though she was marrying an ogre. Mr. Baker would always treat her well, of that she was convinced.

As she suspected, Mr. Baker made no effort to find, or even look over, the books in the library. Standing near the center of the room, with empty chairs all around and the grand windows raining winter sunlight onto them, Mr. Baker turned and faced her, taking both of her hands into his.

"Miss Spencer"—

He apparently *did* remember her true name. With all the sweet endearments he'd been using, she half suspected he'd forgotten it altogether.

—"I know it comes as no surprise that I find you all that is lovely and sweet."

"Thank you, Mr. Baker." Helena forced the words out.

"Almost since the first moment I entered Hedgewood Manor, I felt deeply that I'd found my future companion at last."

Helena's stomach rolled most uncomfortably. She pursed her lips, willing the nausea to subside. He was a good man. She could do far worse.

Remaining without a family, penniless for the rest of her life, certainly would be a lot worse.

"Ah, my dear plum pudding, rest assured that in the future years, you will never know hunger or loneliness."

Isn't that what she wanted? A safe home. Family. Mr. Baker was offering her all of that.

But would he ever be the family she sought? Hadn't she confessed to Fredrick during the ball that she didn't just want a marriage? Any husband was not enough. She wanted someone who cherished her. Someone who would brighten her days and be her safe place to land when it all got to be too hard.

Marriage for the sake of marriage is what she had first set out to obtain—what she'd schemed for with Emma, Eleanor, and Christina. Even Fredrick had helped. But now, staring at exactly who she'd aspired to find, Helena could not deny that in her heart, she knew it wasn't enough. Perhaps she was selfish and would die alone after all. But *this*—what existed between herself and Mr. Baker, good man though he was—it wasn't enough.

"Thank you, sir," she began.

How did one turn down a perfectly reasonable offer from a kind man? In all her planning and late-night talks with Emma, they never once had discussed this outcome.

"I want you to know that I *do* appreciate your attentiveness and generosity. However—"

The library door banged open.

"What is the meaning of this?"

Helena startled at the noise and whirled around. Fredrick stomped into the room, his gaze moving quickly between her and Mr. Baker, his brow etching into a deeper and deeper scowl.

"Baker, I demand an explanation."

Mr. Baker, for his part, only smiled more. "I am to be congratulated, nephew. It seems I will once again be the happiest of men."

Oh, no. No, she hadn't answered him. He was putting words in her mouth. "Please, sir, I have given no answer."

Mr. Baker only patted her hands, still clutched within his

own. "Is not Miss Spencer the loveliest being you have ever met?"

"She is precisely that," Fredrick said, his tone still harsh.

All of Helena's churning insides stilled and then began to hum with a new excitement.

Fredrick stood tall, his hands behind his back. "And so, I want to hear it from *her*. However, if she has not yet *actually* accepted you, Baker, then she needs to know that I intend to offer for her as well."

"Really?" She nearly gasped the word.

Fredrick's scowl softened, and the corner of his lips pulled up. "Yes, Helena. I want to marry you."

A heated thrill rushed through her. Taking the two steps necessary, she threw her arms around him.

"If you'll have me, that is," Fredrick added with a chuckle.

Helena couldn't stop the smile threatening to split her face. She pulled back, looking up into those dark brown eyes she'd come to adore so much. "I've missed having a family so dreadfully, Fredrick. I want nothing more than for you to be my new family."

He tipped his head down, resting his forehead against hers. "I love you, Helena. I love you more than I could ever say."

The tingling joy and burning elation was nearly overwhelming. "I love you too, Fredrick." But instead of wasting time on more words, she pushed up and her lips met his.

He pulled her close, his mouth working over hers. Helena held him close, her fingers moving through his hair. The feel of his hands across her back was one she would never forget.

A soft chuckle pulled them apart.

Good heavens, she'd all but forgotten Mr. Baker.

When Helena looked over at him, he was smiling. "Well," he said with a laugh, "it's about time." Then he turned toward the library door and called out, "You can come in now. He's finally proposed."

The door swung open, and Lady Chapman hurried inside, Eleanor and Christina right behind her. She took one look at Helena and Fredrick in one another's arms and clasped her hands together, hugging them tightly to her chest.

"Praises be," she exclaimed, her smile ever broader than Mr. Baker's. "It's a Christmas Eve miracle."

"Mother?" Fredrick asked.

"Oh come now," Lady Chapman said. "You don't suppose you and your sisters are the only family members who know how to set a trap?"

Fredrick seemed shocked, his sisters no less so.

Lady Chapman glanced over them all, a hint of indignation coloring her features and tone. "Where do you think you all learned it?"

Eleanor and Christina only laughed at this.

But Fredrick's brow dropped again. "So, Baker . . . all his attentions toward Helena . . . ?"

Lady Chapman's expression only grew more triumphant. "All part of my plan. One that my late husband's brother was only too happy to help with."

Mr. Baker bowed Helena's direction. "I hope you can forgive an old man. After what happened this summer, I was terribly downcast. I know I am more than guilty for all you endured. When Lady Chapman wrote to me and explained all, nothing could have stopped me from seeing the both of you happy."

Helena held on to Fredrick, her world shifting about faster than she could keep up with. "So the attentions . . . your proposal?"

"All a means of showing Fredrick what he should have realized weeks ago."

Fredrick's arms tightened around her. "That I can't live without you."

Mr. Baker nodded. "Though I must say, I am glad the ruse

is up. If I had to think up one more dessert to call you by, Miss Spencer, I would have made *myself* sick."

Helena laughed. The emotions swirling inside her were so numerous, she could barely keep up with them all.

Fredrick lowered his head, his mouth coming tantalizingly close to her ear. "Are you sure you want to marry into this ridiculous family?"

Family. She wouldn't have to wait long at all now before she had one again. "You mean a mother who loves you wholeheartedly, sisters who care for others to the point of putting themselves second, and an uncle who is kind and thoughtful? I suppose I could tolerate such an arrangement."

"Oh!" Christina exclaimed. "I've been hoping for the last three weeks that you two would make a match of it."

"Only the last three weeks?" Lady Chapman said. "I've known they were perfect for one another since Miss Spencer put pepper in Fredrick's coffee."

More laughter filled the room even as Helena felt her face grow warm. "You knew about that?"

"Don't worry. No one *told* me. I doubt anyone else pieced together what actually happened that morning. But I am a mother, and I see more than my children will ever know."

Everyone laughed at that. Then, among cheers and shouts, Eleanor and Christina hurried forward, wrapping their arms around Helena and Fredrick. Lady Chapman and Mr. Baker, too, moved forward and joined in the rapturous celebration.

All the while, as they talked over one another, each declaring how perfect a couple they made, Helena basked in the feel of Fredrick's arm around her, his nearness so wonderfully right.

Never would she be alone.

She had a family again.

CHAPTER TWENTY-FIVE

Angry shouts came from the corridor beyond the library, putting an abrupt end to the celebration Helena and the Chapman family were enjoying.

Lord Ellis's voice could be heard above all else. "You blathering, mindless fool!"

Fredrick pressed a quick kiss to Helena's forehead and then hurried toward the library door.

"Calm down, Lord Ellis." Lord Andrews's voice was heard next. "Let us talk about this like gentlemen."

Helena followed quickly after her intended. Her *intended*. La, how wonderful that sounded. Eleanor and Christina trailed directly behind her. Fredrick opened the door and Helena caught sight of the two men standing with fists at their sides.

Mr. Andrews's jaw was tight. "Get a hold of yourself. Come back to my study and we will talk about this—"

"You're an idiot, Andrews," Lord Ellis seethed. "To think I'd simply sit around and *talk* when *your servants* are out there with my horse."

There was so much commotion about them. Helena reached the door and, standing close to Fredrick, she could see every guest gathered about the corridor, save those who stood in the library behind her. Some shuffled about nervously, others decried that Lord Ellis ought to leave if he was going to speak to their host in such a way.

"They were naught but two small children," Lord Andrews said. "No one could have suspected they were capable of this."

"Well, you clearly should have!" Lord Ellis roared.

Amid cries of "what's happened?" Lord Andrews explained while Lord Ellis paced the corridor and muttered to himself.

"I was informed this morning that two of the servants have disappeared in the middle of the night. It seems they have taken a bit of silver with them as well as Lord Ellis's horse."

Cries of disbelief echoed about the space. Helena slipped up closer to Lord Andrews.

"Pardon me, sir, but are you speaking of the new scullery maid and her brother? I believe he was put to work in the stables."

His brow dropped in question. "The very ones. How did you know?"

She only shook her head and stepped back toward Fredrick; her stomach was far too sour to speak more. The joy of moments ago was replaced with worry. Why would the two have done such a thing? They had a warm bed at night and food in their stomachs while working here. Why leave that, even for the money that could be earned by selling some silver and Lord Ellis's horse?

And how did two children expect to be able to sell such a thing on their own?

"I demand to know all," Lord Ellis said. "Where's the housekeeper who hired the two? I want to hear her account."

Apparently, so did the rest of the gathered party. Soon the housekeeper was summoned and requested to recite all that had led to Mary and Jim being employed.

Looking rather pale and far less sure of herself than Helena had ever seen her before, the housekeeper began. "One evening, just before the house party began, I was told a man was at the servants' door wishing to speak with me. He had two children with him, said they were his niece and nephew—"

"Was his name Mr. Chant?" Helena broke in.

All eyes moved to her.

"Well, yes." The housekeeper looked flustered for a moment. "Yes, I believe that is the name he gave me. He said that the children's parents had only just passed, unexpectedly, and that he wanted to keep the children but needed a couple of months to get his affairs in order. He asked if they could work for room and board for a spell. I normally would have turned them away, but with so many visitors coming, I knew we would be a bit short-handed, and the man assured me it would only be temporary."

"It was temporary, all right," Lord Ellis sneered. "Just long enough to fool you all into turning your backs on them."

Noise swelled around Helena. Mrs. Wynn and Lady Chapman insisted that this was not the sort of thing discussed among ladies. Miss Wynn decried that the Andrews were fools to have ever believed two children. Lord Ellis ranted on that he'd been wronged while Lord Andrews urged him to calm down with the support of Eleanor, Christina, and Topper.

Helena remained apart from the group.

Fredrick's hand slowly rubbed the small of her back in gentle circles and Helena leaned more fully against him. How had she become so blessed as to have a man who both helped her be positive but also allowed her the time to be sorrowful when she needed it?

"Poor Mary and Jim," she said softly. "Why do you suppose they did it?"

She felt Fredrick shrug beneath her. "For the money, I would assume."

Helena thought back over the few conversations she'd had with the children and rehearsed to herself what the housekeeper had said.

Realization struck and she stood up straight. Turning, she faced Fredrick. "The housekeeper said Mr. Chant claimed the children's parents had *only just* passed away, but Mary told me their parents died three years ago this winter."

"Which means Mr. Chant was in on it. This was the plan from the beginning."

Lord Andrews's voice sailed up and over the gathered party. "There are still enough horses in my stables for every man. If we set out now, I firmly believe we can catch the little devils before they've gone any further."

With shouts of agreement, all the men charged from the room. Helena's heart beat fast; there was no doubt in her mind that if—or rather when—Mary and Jim were caught, they'd be sent to the workhouses or even debtor's prison.

Since they'd stolen a horse, there was a real chance they could even be hanged. Helena had read more than one article stating children as young as twelve had been hanged for various crimes.

Helena took hold of Fredrick's arm. "Mr. Chant must have forced them to do it. Mary confided in me that he hurts them often. I don't think Mary and Jim are to blame; Mr. Chant probably left them no choice."

"Lord Ellis won't see it that way."

The men were already moving down the corridor and toward the entryway.

"Which is why I have to find them first." Helena pushed off him. She could slip up to her bedchamber, be into her riding habit in less than ten minutes, and then have a horse saddled.

"Oh no." Fredrick took hold of both her arms. "It's too dangerous. Besides, there will be far too many questions if any of the gentlemen catch sight of you, out on horseback, when you're supposed to be recovering from last night. If Lord Ellis even suspects you wish to hide those two from him, he will do everything possible to stop you. He very well may brand you a horse thief along with them."

That was true. If she went out, she'd have to not only find Mary and Jim *first*, she'd have to do it without anyone else seeing her.

"I can't sit back and do nothing," she said.

"I'll go. My presence will be easily explained. I'm simply one more of the party searching for the stolen horse. They won't know I'm actually going to protect Mary and Jim. Besides, I'm already dressed for a cold ride." He motioned to the greatcoat he wore and his thick riding boots.

Helena's eyes burned with hot tears. She threw her arms around his neck. "Thank you."

He hugged her close. "Anything for you, my dearest love."

"It seems scandal follows me wherever I go."

He only hugged her tighter. "So long as you allow me to go with you, too, I couldn't care less." He gave her a quick kiss and then was off.

CHAPTER TWENTY-SIX

Helena sat beside Christina, sipping her after-dinner tea, but couldn't focus on the conversation around her. All the Christmas Eve plans had been canceled since none of the gentlemen were back. For most of dinner, Lady Chapman had triumphantly discussed her son's betrothal to "that sweet Miss Spencer." Helena had wondered so many times what it would be like to have a mother—one who was kind and proud of her—and now, it seemed, she finally had her wish.

If only she could enjoy it.

She *would* enjoy it, she was certain. For years to come, she would be blessed with a dear mother-in-law who loved her as any mother loved a daughter. But for tonight, she was too wrapped up in worry for Mary and Jim. Not a word, not a message, nothing had been brought to the ladies.

Not even Fredrick had sent word to her.

"More tea, Miss Spencer?" Lady Andrews asked.

Helena looked down at her cup. It was empty. She couldn't even remember lifting the thing to her lips; she must have drunk it absently. Her stomach was suddenly overly full and nauseous. "No, thank you." She placed the cup and saucer onto an obliging table.

"You don't suppose they've met with an accident, do you?" Christina whispered as the other women continued their conversation. "It is quite snowy outside."

"I'm sure they are all fine." Helena tried to pour a little consolation into her friend, but the truth was, she was so overwrought thinking of Mary and Jim that she could barely keep her own nerves from fraying into a thousand pieces.

She could always retire. A little quiet and solitude sounded heavenly right now. But suppose word *did* come from Fredrick? She might not hear if she was abed. So she sat.

The women talked of Christmas Eves long past.

They spoke of winter games and snowy adventures.

Finally, Miss Wynn was prevailed upon to play a bit at the pianoforte for them all. It seemed they'd all quite run out of things to say, yet no one wanted to go to bed before hearing the outcome of the gentlemen's search.

As Miss Wynn began the second movement of her song, Willis moved up beside Helena.

"Lord Chapman is here to see you, miss," he whispered low enough only she would hear.

"Thank you." Helena waited until Willis had left the room, then glanced about herself. No one seemed to be aware of her, so she stood and hurried as fast as she could without making a sound.

Willis, who'd remained near the door, showed her to the parlor.

Fredrick stood, his shoulders brushed with snow and his face red from the cold.

He greeted her but waited until they were alone—the door left open for propriety—before he spoke. "I've found them," he said in a rush. "I've told them to wait near where the lane to Hedgewood Manor meets the main road. I'm taking Lord

Ellis's horse the opposite direction. I'll leave him where it'll look like he broke free on his own and wandered off." He stretched a bag out to her. "Hide the silver somewhere here, in the house." As she took it, he held out a letter to her. "Then give this to my valet."

Helena took the slip of paper and read it over quickly.

I need you to ready a small buggy for Miss Spencer. She has a quick errand to make. No one is to know of this. Speak of it to no one.

"After you hide the silver," Fredrick hurried on, "go for Mary and Jim. With both the horse and silver found, I'm hoping everyone will assume the children were runaways and not thieves."

Helena held the silver in one hand and the letter in the other. "There are a lot of ways this could go wrong."

"I know, but I'll keep the other men away from the road."

"I can't bring Mary and Jim back here. If they're found, they would still face dire consequences."

His lips pulled to the side as his brow dropped. "I don't have any acquaintances in the area and know of nowhere they might hide for the night."

It was moments like this when one needed family most. "My uncle," Helena said. "He lives in Dunwell. That's not too far." She remembered the way. After picking up the children, she could head straight there.

"Are you sure he would take them in, even just for one night?"

He probably wouldn't. No, the more she thought on it, the more certain she was that he absolutely *would not* take them in. "I shall have to stay and convince him."

Fredrick's worried expression softened. "I pity the man who tries to defy you."

Helena nodded sagely. "I may have to put pepper in his tea."

Fredrick chuckled softly, then his expression softened. "Are you certain you're strong enough for this? After last night?"

"Strong enough to help two small children? I'm hurt you had to ask."

His smile returned and he hugged her to him. "I'll see to the horse and make sure you have plenty of time to gather Mary and Jim and take them to your uncle's. Then I'll meet you there."

With a kiss to her forehead, he charged back into the cold, dark evening.

Helena moved toward the stairs. She would speak with his valet first, get the man started on the horse and buggy, and then hide the silver someplace unexpected yet easily found tomorrow morning as the maids cleaned.

Then she would brave the winter night herself.

FREDRICK'S VALET SEEMED CURIOUS ABOUT THE NOTE HELENA gave him and even more so when, after reading it, Helena asked to borrow a spare greatcoat and man's hat. However, Fredrick was right to trust him. The man asked no questions and soon presented Helena with a well-hitched buggy just as soon as she had seen to the matter of the silver.

Dressed in the greatcoat and hat, she stepped up into the buggy. Hopefully, she would appear as a man from a distance. She'd snagged a few things from the kitchen beneath the bench where they wouldn't fly out during the ride—a little milk and a bit of cake. Then, she arranged the thick blanket over her lap and righted the man's wide-brim hat. Thank goodness for the two hot stones at her feet. The long sleeves of Fredrick's greatcoat hung down past her hands, making the handling of the reins a bit tricky. But she was determined to manage.

It seemed the valet's concern finally won out over his sense of propriety, for he said, "Please excuse me, miss, but a lady riding out alone in the middle of the night is highly unusual."

"Thank you for your concern," Helena replied. "I shall be quite all right."

She knew how to handle horses and the buggy was small enough not to be overly difficult, despite her long sleeves.

"I could accompany you myself if you desire it. Or have one of the footmen sent for."

Helena hesitated. It would be nice to have either the valet or a footman with her. Perhaps Willis? It would lend her propriety if she were seen and would be a strong hand if the buggy got caught in the snow. Nonetheless, there wouldn't be room in the small conveyance for two adults and two children.

"No thank you," Helena said, picking up the reins. "I can manage quite well on my own." She gave the reins a gentle snap and the horse started forward. Blessedly, the valet said no more. He merely bowed slightly and stepped aside. Still, Helena could feel his gaze on her as she rode out toward the main road.

She hadn't allowed herself to second guess the plan since the moment she and Fredrick had discussed it. But now that she was alone, with nothing but the cold and the snow clouds for company, she couldn't help but wonder. Suppose she was caught? From a distance, she would look like a man out for a ride. That would offer her some anonymity. But if anyone drew near enough to see her face or the auburn curls that refused to stay tucked up inside the hat, she would be had. Suppose Lord Andrews saw her? He could easily misunderstand her actions as stealing his servants. Or what if another servant, or even another house guest, had seen her leave? They might very well come to the conclusion she was off to a wanton rendezvous. The past several months, Helena had done nothing but try to prove herself pure and above scrutiny. Yet, scandal seemed to follow her everywhere she went, no matter what she did. Well, if that was the price she paid for the safety of Mary and Jim, she would do it ten times over.

She arrived at the turn-off to the main road without incident. She pulled the horse to a stop and listened. The night was perfectly still. Fredrick had said he'd keep the other gentlemen searching the opposite regions of Hedgewood Manor. She could only hope he *kept* them there for a bit longer.

"Mary?" she called softly. "Jim?"

No answer. There was a chance they had not had the opportunity to arrive yet. They were walking, after all, while she'd had the benefit of a buggy. Helena kept her gaze on the turn-off but snuggled under the blanket a bit more. She may be in for a long wait. Bless those two heated stones at her feet, else-wise she was liable to freeze to death waiting. It was a frigid night.

A twig snapped somewhere to her left. Helena sat up straight, the cold air rushing in all around her. She shoved the blanket down closer around her lap as she leaned out of the buggy slightly.

"Hello? It's me, Miss Spencer."

In response to her name, a bush rustled, and out stepped two small forms she easily recognized.

"Come, come." She hurried them over.

Mary and Jim scampered the rest of the way and climbed into the buggy. What a relief it was to finally see them both once more. Helena pulled the blanket off her own lap and tucked it around the two children. They were shivering, the dears. Helena pushed both heated stones underneath their feet.

"Careful," she said, "don't burn your toes, but keep your feet just above them."

Both children nodded. Taking hold of the reins, Helena set them off toward Dunwell. The ride was made in silence. Driving in the dark of night was proving harder than Helena had expected, leaving her little time to think of things to say.

Most likely, Mary and Jim were either too cold or too scared to speak themselves.

They pulled up to Uncle Scrooge's place of business and Helena sighed in relief. There were lights on and a sleigh parked out front. He was still up. She probably should have realized before now that the chances of him still being at work near midnight on Christmas Eve were small, at best. She'd been too wound up to properly consider it. She was lucky he was still there.

Nonetheless, someone else was there as well. She didn't recognize the sleigh. She was fairly sure everyone from Hedgewood Manor who was out searching for Mary and Jim had done so on horseback, not by sleigh, so she wasn't overly worried. But she still couldn't risk anyone seeing them. Clucking to the horses, Helena drove the buggy past Uncle Scrooge's office and down to the first turn in the road. With the blanket and heated stone for the children and herself in a warm greatcoat and thick hat, they would be all right out in the cold for a minute longer. She'd wait for Uncle Scrooge's guest to leave and then they'd go inside and speak with him. She just hoped it wouldn't take all night.

CHAPTER TWENTY-SEVEN

Two individuals, a man and a woman, walked out of Uncle Scrooge's place of business. They stopped for a moment, talking beneath the moonlight. Helena held both children close to her, hushing them softly whenever they opened their mouths or shifted about too much.

The man and woman appeared as though they might kiss but didn't. Then the man helped the woman into the waiting sleigh and climbed in himself before they rode off.

Helena sighed out in relief. That was one difficulty avoided. Leaving the buggy pulled around the corner, she stepped down, snow crunching beneath her boots.

"Come." She beckoned to Mary and Jim, lifting them down, one by one. "Huddle close, under my coat. You'll be warmer that way."

Neither child was dressed warmly enough, in her estimation. Thankfully, the overly large coat Fredrick's valet had secured for her fit around her and both children and could still button without a problem. They shuffled up toward the hole-pocked door. There were footsteps coming from inside, as well as two deep voices. If she wasn't mistaken, the voices were none other than Uncle Scrooge and his assistant, Mr. Cratchit.

Either way, they couldn't stay outside any longer. Helena struck the knocker against the metal plate. The sound echoed in the stillness.

One of the voices said something—Uncle Scrooge grumbling most likely. Well, in this she couldn't fault him. No doubt, he was as opposed to being interrupted in the middle of the night as she would be.

The door swung open a small bit.

"Good evening, Mr. Cratchit," she said, recognizing the bit of white hair and wrinkled eyes that she could see.

"Ah, the lovely Miss Spencer. Come inside. Come inside."

With Mary and Jim each hugging a leg, their heads coming up only to her waist, it was with an awkward shuffle that they moved inside. It was hardly warmer inside the dark and dank entryway. Disappointing, but she probably should have expected as much.

"What was I just saying?" Uncle Scrooge said to Mr. Cratchit from behind his desk. "My niece seems insistent on allowing me no peace at all this Christmas."

"In that, you are wrong, sir," Helena said, keeping an arm around each child beneath her coat. "You said that I have allowed you no peace *this* Christmas. I can assure you, now that we've met, I plan to allow you no peace *any* Christmas from here on out. That is, unless you've changed your mind and wish to join us for Christmas dinner tomorrow?"

"Humbug," he snarled, then sneezed, and then shivered.

"Uncle Scrooge." Helena hurried forward as quickly as the three of them could. "Are you ill?" Now that she drew closer and had a better view of him, his face was drawn and pale. Large red rings hung beneath his eyes, and she thought there was a bit of sweat clinging to his forehead.

"I am perfectly healthy," Uncle Scrooge said.

"It's no wonder," she said, choosing to ignore his blatant lie, "with the room forever cold. Mr. Cratchit," she said, turning around. The smiling man was waiting just behind her. "Go fetch a large heap of firewood. My uncle is far too cold."

"Mr. Cratchit," Uncle Scrooge barked, "don't you dare leave this room!" His eyes caught hold of something, and his head swung back to Helena as though jerked there by a rope.

"I see something strange," Uncle Scrooge said, pointing an accusatory finger toward Helena's feet, "and not belonging to yourself, protruding from your coat."

There was nothing for it. She knew she would have to tell him who she'd brought with her eventually. Helena unbuttoned the coat and pulled it open. Mary and Jim both looked terrified.

Uncle Scrooge responded far more expressively than she'd anticipated. He reeled back, his face going through a series of cringes as though he saw the children as wretched, hideous, or even frightful.

"Are they yours?" he finally croaked out.

"They are some man's natural children, but I know not whose."

"Then what have you to do with them?"

Anger that he would treat them so callously boiled up inside her. "Are there no prisons? Is that what you mean? Are there no workhouses?" If he chose to ignore and rebuff her, so be it. But that he was so abjectly against caring for two children who were alone in the world—it was nearly enough to make her want to scream. At the very least, it made her want to spin around and leave him to his icy room and fever.

But no, her time here may prove to be short—she certainly hoped it would be—but until Fredrick came, she would make the most of this situation. Despite all her senses contradicting the notion, Helena still believed there was good in Uncle Scrooge. Somewhere. Deep, *deep* inside.

"Jim," she said, turning to the small boy, "you and Mary go help Mr. Cratchit fetch some firewood. This room needs warming up, no matter what my uncle says."

This time, Uncle Scrooge merely grumbled beneath his breath.

"Come, children," Mr. Cratchit said, happily showing them the way. "We will make a right proper Christmas Eve fire, after all."

The two children followed the old man. With them gone, Helena found she had little more to say to her uncle. She silently took the same chair she'd sat in before.

Her mind, however, followed Mary and Jim from the room. She'd secreted them away from Hedgewood Manor, all right. But what now? And how soon would Fredrick return? She ached for his reassuring presence.

Soon, she learned there was no cause to worry for the children. They'd left looking unsure but returned with arms full of wood and smiles on their faces.

"And then, strangest of all," Mr. Cratchit was saying as they entered the room, "my grandson, Tim, replied that he hoped the people saw him in the church, because he was a cripple, and it might be pleasant to them to remember upon Christmas Day he who made lame beggars walk, and blind men see."

"What a strange thing to say," Mary replied.

"Ah, yes," Mr. Cratchit said. "He gets thoughtful sitting by himself so much. I suppose he can think up some strange things now and then. But his heart is as good as gold, it is."

Jim, appearing bored with the conversation, hurried over to Helena. "Look at all the wood!" He held his small share out toward her.

"Excellent." Helena smiled down at him. Then she directed them all on how to build a blazing fire, and soon the room was warming up.

Still, Uncle Scrooge took to shivering.

"Uncle," Helena said once the fire was well in hand, "You ought to go lie down. You look terrible."

"Some familial love," he scoffed. "Telling an old man he looks terrible."

Mr. Cratchit, however, moved up close to Helena and whispered. "That he's allowed you to warm the room is a miracle. His bedchamber upstairs is even colder than this room was when you entered."

"Will he not permit us to light a fire in there as well?" she asked, equally as soft.

Uncle Scrooge swayed gently in his chair. Though there were no other sounds in the room besides herself and Mr. Cratchit speaking, she still was not fully sure Uncle Scrooge was in a right enough mind to listen in.

"I've tried every night this winter," Mr. Cratchit said. "He hasn't allowed it yet."

"Very well; it's probably best if he stays down here then. Perhaps you could go fetch him some blankets, perhaps even a pillow from his room?"

"At once, miss." Mr. Cratchit gave her a shaking bow and then strode toward the door. He turned back before disappearing from the room. "And then, perhaps, you might sit with him for a while as I go fetch my granddaughter? She knows a thing or two about caring for a fever."

"Of course."

Mr. Cratchit nodded his gratitude and then left.

Mary and Jim sat next to the fire, their little hands stretched out toward the heat. It wasn't exactly a merry Christmas Eve. But Helena was determined to make the most of it.

"How about we play some games?" she asked, loud enough for Mary and Jim, as well as her uncle, to hear.

"Whatever for?" Uncle Scrooge argued.

"Because it is Christmas Eve, and one ought to be jolly, tonight of all nights."

"What should we play?" Mary asked.

"How, When, Where!" yelled Jim.

"All right, Jim. You go first," Helena said.

Uncle Scrooge only grumbled as Helena and Mary asked Jim the three questions: "How do you like it?", to which Jim replied, "hot, but cold is good, too"; "When do you like it?", to which he said, "all the time, but I've never had it for breakfast, so I'm only imagining it would be delicious then, too"; and finally, "Where do you like it?"

"Anywhere I happen to be at the moment," Jim said with a grin.

Helena pursed her lips in thought, turning to Mary. "What do you think? It sounds like he's thinking of something to eat."

"His favorite food is cake," Mary replied.

"Is it cake?" Uncle Scrooge asked Jim.

Helena was shocked into momentary silence. Jim, bless the boy, didn't so much as bat an eye that the grouchy old man was suddenly, unexpectedly, engaging in the game.

"Yes!" Jim said with joy. "Specifically, honey cake while it's still hot."

"Yum." Mary sighed.

Helena found her own mouth watering, too. She would have to be sure and have the dessert made up so these two could be given large slices as soon as she was able. Perhaps Mr. Baker would help her? He clearly had an affinity for sweets, after all.

Mr. Cratchit returned, his arms full of soft fabrics. Helena directed him as they placed a pillow behind Uncle Scrooge's back and two blankets over his lap. Another blanket was placed on the floor for the children.

With a quick and wordless "thank you," Mr. Cratchit slipped out the door.

As he left, Helena turned back toward the room just in time to see Uncle Scrooge sigh, almost contentedly, as he settled. Helena smiled inwardly. Others might have thought her foolish to believe her uncle could be more than miserly, but tonight was proof that they were wrong.

Uncle Scrooge spoke even with his eyes closed. "Mary's turn to think up something for us to guess."

The little girl was only too delighted, and on the games continued.

FREDRICK ARGUED WITH HIMSELF THE ENTIRE TIME HE WAS ON horseback. Helena had left a message with his valet detailing where to find her uncle's place of business. He only hoped she was truly there. If the old man was as hard-hearted as he'd been made out to be, he very well might have turned Helena and the two children away.

It had been hours since he'd spoken to her last, far longer than he'd originally anticipated their separation to be. But Lord Ellis had been stubbornly determined to find Mary and Jim. Even well after Fredrick knew Helena had gathered the children and taken them away, Lord Ellis insisted they search. They found his horse—as Fredrick had planned—and *still*, Lord Ellis drove them all to continue the hunt for the missing children. The longer the night wore on, the more certain Fredrick felt that spiriting the children away had been the right thing to do.

Finally, well after midnight, Lord Andrews persuaded Lord Ellis to be done for the night. Fredrick had silently thanked the heavens their host had said something. Fredrick had wanted to long before but worried it would have drawn too much attention to himself if he were the one to recommend they cry off. After that, of course, he had to see to a place to keep the children hidden for a few days. Lord Adley, whose ball had been quite fine a few weeks ago, was the only person Fredrick could think of who lived close enough and whose generous disposition could be counted on. Though the butler had protested waking Lord Adley at all, once Fredrick was able to explain to the man, he'd agreed to help immediately.

Now, only a few minutes before two in the morning, Fredrick finally pulled his horse to a stop before a weather-beaten building. The door was atrocious, with enough light pouring through it to make him aware of two things at once: first, that the door could not possibly be keeping all the cold out, causing him to worry Helena, Mary, and Jim had been freezing these past several hours, and two, that so much light meant people were certainly up even at this late hour.

He neared the door and the sound of hearty laughter greeted him. Well—that was not at all what he'd worried he would find. He knocked softly, but when the laughter continued and no one answered the door, he simply opened it himself.

The sight off to his right was not at all what he'd imagined when Helena had first suggested she hide at her uncle's place of business. Helena sat in a rickety old chair, but she was leaned forward, clearly engaged in whatever they were doing. The two children sat on a blanket on the floor, their faces alight with excitement. Even a wrinkled man, who he assumed must be Helena's Uncle Scrooge, sat bundled up in blankets with something almost akin to a smile on his face.

Fredrick moved quietly into the room. They were discussing amongst themselves what it could possibly be that Mary liked best with flowers on it, when the weather was fine, and whenever she went to church. They each held small glasses with some kind of drink inside and seemed quite cheerful.

Helena called out several responses. "A hat? Fine shoes?"

All the while Jim, too, was yelling, "A dog? A horse?"

Even Uncle Scrooge seemed unable to resist. "A spencer jacket? A parasol? Really now, Helena, whoever heard of putting flowers on shoes?"

Helena only huffed. "Well, one *might* embroider them on." She finally caught sight of Fredrick and waved him over.

He moved to stand behind her.

Her whole face was lit up. "Thank you for helping tonight," she said softly.

He wrapped an arm about her shoulder and hugged her to him. "Are you ready to go?"

"Not yet." Her voice turned even lower. "We have to wait for Mr. Cratchit and his granddaughter to return."

"Who?"

"I'll explain later."

"I know," Jim called out. "A dress!"

"That's it!" Mary giggled.

On they played for several more minutes before the front door opened and two individuals hurried in, a white-haired man and a young woman probably close to Helena's age with dark hair. The woman turned toward them, her eyes growing wide at the sight of Mr. Scrooge playing with two children.

The white-haired man, however, only smiled more as he approached Fredrick and clapped him on the shoulder. "My granddaughter is here now. Thank you for staying with him."

"Happy to be of service," Fredrick said, then turned to Helena and silently asked if she was ready to go.

Helena nodded that she was and turned back to the children. "All right, Mary and Jim. It's time for us to leave. Tell Mr. Scrooge thank you for a fine Christmas Eve."

Only adding shock to surprise, Uncle Scrooge called out, "One half-hour more. Only one. Come, we can play a new game. Yes and No."

"I am sorry," Helena said, "but we truly should be leaving."

"Are Christmas Eve visits so short?" Mr. Scrooge seemed actually displeased by the notion.

Helena gave Fredrick a look which clearly indicated she was as surprised as he at her uncle's response.

"I'm afraid tonight has been brief," she said. "But Christmas Eve actually ended at midnight and it is already well after two in the morning."

Uncle Scrooge grumbled something to himself, but that transformed into a yawn almost immediately. "I suppose it is rather late."

Both Mary and Jim yawned in response; Fredrick had to stifle a yawn himself.

"Ha!" Uncle Scrooge cried out suddenly, pointing at each of them who'd yawned. "I would have won at Forfeits, don't claim that I wouldn't have."

Helena laughed and moved up beside him. "Sharp as a needle, you are, Uncle Scrooge." Bending down, she kissed him atop his head.

Uncle Scrooge actually blushed a bit at the kiss, every bit as much as he squirmed under the show of affection.

"Don't forget," Helena said, "Christmas dinner tomorrow."

A touch of surliness returned to Uncle Scrooge's expression. "Bah." He shrugged her away.

Helena pursed her lips but eventually walked back over to Fredrick.

"Give him time," Fredrick whispered to her. "I rather believe this is the merriest he's been in years, if not decades. A change like that does not usually happen all at once."

Helena nodded as she moved to the front door with Mary and Jim.

Fredrick watched her pull back on an old greatcoat of his, one that the tailor had made rather too big, even for him. It enveloped her, and then, in turn, fully hid both the children.

The way it dangled down over her hands was nothing short of charming.

"Coming?" she asked.

"Give me a minute with your uncle."

"We'll just get situated in the buggy."

Once they'd slipped out into the night, Fredrick hurried back over to Uncle Scrooge. He didn't want to keep Helena or the children out in the cold for very long, but he did have something he wanted to ask the man in private.

"Sir," Fredrick began, "I have a matter of some importance to discuss."

Uncle Scrooge's head lolled a bit to the side, his scowl emphasizing the many wrinkles across his face. "Well? Out with it."

This was the Uncle Scrooge he'd expected to meet. All callous gruffness.

"Sir, I wish to ask for your permission to marry Helena. I understand you are her nearest relation, and I felt it only proper for me to speak with you on the matter."

Uncle Scrooge only grunted in return.

"Don't be angry," Fredrick pressed, "Say we have your blessing, and then you can spend every Christmas Eve in as merry a way as this one for the rest of your days."

"Why should I?"

"Why not? You've enjoyed tonight—don't say you haven't—and I should think you'd like to—"

"Balderdash. I mean, why *marry* the girl in the first place?"

There was only one answer he could give to that. "Because I fell in love."

"Fell in love?" growled Scrooge. "Why, that's the only thing in the world more ridiculous than a merry Christmas. Be off with you now." He pulled the blanket about him even tighter, slouching down into the chair.

If Fredrick wasn't wrong, the man was ill and growing worse.

Still, he didn't feel he could leave without some kind of an answer. It would mean much to Helena to know Fredrick had gotten her grouchy uncle's approval. "Please, say you will bless the marriage. A single word from you is all I'm asking, and then I'll be on my way, and you will be reassured of having many more jolly Christmas Eves in the future."

"Very well," Scrooge said. "Go and marry the girl already, but leave me in peace!"

"Thank you, sir." Fredrick bowed and then spun about to leave. Still, just before walking out the door, he motioned Mr. Cratchit over. "He seems in quite a bad way. I'd strongly recommend you send for the doctor straight away."

"My granddaughter will know what to do. She's nursed many a fever. Don't you worry; we'll see to him."

"Very good." Though Uncle Scrooge was a crotchety man, Fredrick would never forget that even *he* still had a spark of merriment in him—though how Helena had managed to draw it out, he would never know. That she, of all people, could do so was not surprising, and he loved her all the more for it.

He stepped outside and found Helena and the children sitting very stiffly in the buggy.

"Did you see him?" Jim asked the moment Fredrick brought his horse around.

"Who?" Now that he was closer to them, he could see that both Helena and Mary looked a touch on edge.

"Don't worry." Helena's voice sounded strained as well. "I am sure he's just a gentleman from round-abouts."

Jim, however, with wide eyes and a bit of a mischievous smile about his lips leaned out of the buggy and nearer Fredrick. "It's the grim reaper. I swear it." He pointed with a hand down the road.

Fredrick followed the direction the boy indicated, turning

fully around. Sure enough, down the road, just past Uncle Scrooge's place of business, stood a man dressed fully in black. His large shoulders and tall form seemed to bespeak of a hapless fate.

"We should go," Helena said.

Fredrick agreed. He didn't know who the man was, he couldn't see a bit of his face, but he was more than willing to leave if the man was headed their way.

Securing his horse to the side of the buggy, he climbed inside. There wasn't truly enough room, so Jim sat on Helena's lap and Mary on his. Fredrick called to the horse pulling the buggy and they started forward.

As they passed the strange man, Fredrick gave him one last look. The man seemed to be watching them drive by. Fredrick tipped his hat at the man. In return, the man slowly inclined his head. Still, Fredrick could not make out a single feature of his face.

Turning, the man walked toward Uncle Scrooge's place of business, the night's blackness enveloping him almost immediately.

The moment no one could see the unsettling man, they all relaxed a bit. Soon, due to the late hour and the rocking of the buggy, no doubt, both children were sleeping.

"What a strange night," Helena said, resting her head against Fredrick's shoulder.

"Nothing across this whole globe will ever strike me as being as unexpected as your uncle joining in those games. You're a wonder, you are."

She laughed. "So long as I'm *your* wonder, it's all right by me."

"You always will be."

She sighed a contented sigh.

"I asked him for permission to marry you," he said.

"Oh?"

"I think we have your cheerful optimism to thank, but he said yes."

She settled in closer to him. "How divine."

"And I told him he can expect many more jolly Christmas Eves in the future."

"I should like that." She sounded nearly asleep.

"I spoke with Lord Adley before coming to meet you. He's agreed to hide the children for a time. I say we post the banns and get married as soon as possible. Then we can have Mary and Jim come stay with us."

"And Jim will have honey cake and Mary as many dresses as she could ever want."

Fredrick smiled. "You all *three* will have anything and everything your hearts desire."

"Thank you." The words slurred together.

"You will like my estate near Wilmslow. It won't take long to get there. I think a person could take years to get to know the wild woods about it and never get bored. And we—"

She snored softly.

Fredrick chuckled. "But that can all wait for another time." Leaning over, careful not to disrupt Mary still on his lap, Fredrick kissed the top of Helena's head.

"Merry Christmas, my love."

EPILOGUE

Three Months Later

Helena was back in the hedge maze. She turned first one way and then another, but no matter which turn she took, she seemed no closer to escape. There had to be a way out. There had to be some path she'd not yet taken. The dark shadow she knew was coming slipped over the path in front of her. Helena tried to stifle her scream but couldn't. Suppose it heard her? Suppose something else equally as bad heard? She clamped both hands over her mouth.

Warm, comforting arms wrapped around her, hugging her close.

"It's all right, Helena," said a deep, familiar voice. "It's only a nightmare."

Fredrick?

"Wake up. You're safe, my love."

The hedge maze faded around her, and she was in her bed once more. Her hands trembled, and she was breathing fast, but Fredrick's arms around her calmed her racing heart.

"Shh," he said, pulling her still closer to him, his own voice drowsy from sleep. "You're safe with me, dearest."

She held his arms close about her, and for several minutes did nothing but breathe in and out. After a few minutes, she relaxed.

"The hedge maze again?" he asked.

"Yes. I really wish the pointless nightmares would stop." At least this one hadn't included Mr. Chant.

"So do I," he said with a yawn. For weeks, Mr. Chant had been the shadow hiding among the hedges. Eventually, he'd been located but had escaped to America before being caught. She could not express how relieved she had been that she never had to fear him coming after the children. A small bit of a smile pulled at her lips, and she turned over, facing her husband. "At least I'm not alone anymore, not even in my nightmares."

"You've a family now—albeit one that doesn't seem to understand when they need to take themselves off."

"Oh, come now, your mother and sisters are welcome to stay here with us for as long as they desire."

"I just wish they'd want to spend some time at another one of my holdings. What's the point of being an earl and having more than one house if we can't send my family to another one so you and I can be alone *together* for a bit?"

"You wouldn't dream of asking them to leave; admit it. Besides, I've been without family for a long time, and I've never had a mother or sisters. I'd be very sad if you sent them away already. I cannot tell you how much fun it's been to help *my sister* plan her wedding."

He sighed, shifting about on the bed to get more comfortable. "Very well. They can stay. But only until Christina is wed. After that, I make no promises."

If she truly thought he would kick out his own mother and Eleanor once Christina was gone, she might be worried. But when it came to the women in his life, Fredrick was generous to a fault. Helena kissed his cheek. "You are a good son. Everything your father hoped you'd become and more."

"That's because I have a bit of sunshine right beside me every step of the way."

"Who, Mary and Jim?" she asked innocently. Even several weeks later, she could not believe he'd agreed when she'd asked him if they could raise the two children as their own. She had been very blessed the day Mr. Baker and Lord Shakerley had entwined hers and Fredrick's lives together.

"No. *You*, you troublemaker."

"I take offense at that. I haven't put pepper in your tea *once* since the wedding."

"Don't think I didn't know it was you who stuck hothouse flowers all around and in my horse's saddle and bridle."

"But you were so uptight—"

"I was getting *married*."

"—I had to do *something* to get you to loosen up."

Fredrick laughed. "He did look ridiculous, didn't he?"

"Your mother laughed so hard, I think she almost cried." It had been a wondrous day.

"Do you know what else is ridiculous?" he asked, drawing her close. His nearness sent her nerves tingling.

"What's that?"

"That pitiful little peck on the cheek you gave me a few minutes ago. I think something that unremarkable could hardly be called a kiss at all."

"Ooh, I think we should fix that." She slipped her hands up his chest and around the back of his neck.

"As do I."

And so they did.

The End
The series continues in
The Peace of Christmas Yet to Come

AFTERWORD

I hope you have enjoyed *The Joy of Christmas Present*. While I only took Charles Dickens's story in essence, I have made many references to the original, particularly to the scenes which transpire during the visit of the second spirit; still, some inspiration also comes from the scene when Scrooge's nephew comes to see him, before Jacob Marley appears and warns Scrooge of his fate.

Characters:

~In Charles Dickens's book, Scrooge's only living family is his nephew, the son of his sister, Fanny. I've switched that so he has a niece instead, but other family members I've left the same. Dickens's book does say that Scrooge and his father did not get along, which was why Scrooge spent so much of his childhood abandoned. Also, Fanny had only one child and died in childbirth.

~I gave Scrooge's niece the name Helena because it means "light" or "joyful." Also, in Dickens's story, Fred's wife "played properly upon the harp; and played amongst other tunes a simple little air." For this reason, I have Helena playing the harp in this story. Another character trait I took from Dickens's Fred and gave to Helena is Fred's insistence that there is good in his Uncle. Fred never stops believing that Scrooge can still be happy and generous again one day.

~Fred is the name of Scrooge's nephew in Dickens's story. I wanted to keep the name, so that's how Lord Chapman got his first name.

~Topper comes directly from Dickens's story. We don't know much about him other than his name and that he is quite in love with the sister of Fred's wife. In this book, I kept both Topper and the sister; I only made her Lord Chapman's sister, instead of Helena's. Moreover, Topper gifting the sister a necklace and a ring also comes straight from the book. I feel it's unclear in Dickens's book if the ring is meant as an engagement ring or not, but it is clear that Topper is completely taken with the sister and doesn't care to be a bachelor any longer.

~Once more, there are Mr. Marley and Mr. Scrooge in this story. However, since there is still a book to come, I will hold off, yet again, from saying more here.

Scenes:
~Much of Scrooge's time with the Ghost of Christmas Present is spent at his nephew's Christmas party. It's there, among friends, music, and laughter, that Scrooge begins to remember the joy of life. This inspired me to place The Joy of Christmas Present at a house party.

~More still, it's the many times that music is mentioned in Dickens's book that caused me to bring it up many times in this one. Speaking of Scrooge's nephew, Dickens writes:

"For they were a musical family, and knew what they were about, when they sung a Glee or Catch . . . especially Topper, who could growl away in the bass like a good one . . ."

As an aside, a Catch is similar to a round, where one person starts and then others join in later.

~When Helena visits her Uncle Scrooge on Christmas Eve night, I built the scene based on a couple of different lines in Dickens's story (both taken from during the time of the second spirit). The first is ". . .there is nothing in the world so irresistibly contagious as laughter and good-humour;" and the second, "[Scrooge] begged like a boy to be allowed to stay until the guests departed . . . 'Here is a new game' said Scrooge. 'One half hour, Spirit, only one!'" Dickens even mentions them playing Yes and No, which is why I have Helena, Mary, and Jim play it with Scrooge.

~One of the main themes I wanted to pull from Scrooge's time with the Ghost of Christmas Present is captured well in a conversation Scrooge has with the Spirit near the end:

"'Are spirits' live so short?' asked Scrooge.

"'My life upon this globe, is very brief,' replied the Ghost. 'It ends tonight.'"

I believe one of the best things we can learn from this second spirit is that we all live on this earth but briefly, and so we must make the most of it. It is an inescapable part of life that situations in which we might do good come and go—and once they're gone those opportunities are no longer available. The death of Helena's father and the change in her situation helped her to realize how fleeting life can be. When we see someone in need, it is best to act quickly.

~As Scrooge is traveling with the Ghost of Christmas Present, they come across a miner, a lighthouse keeper, and a captain at sea. Though in Dickens's story the three men are not together, I chose to make them friends and have them meet with Lord Chapman in a local pub. In Dickens's story, these three men serve to help Scrooge see that, no matter one's situation, there is joy to be had. I tried to echo that idea in having my miner, lighthouse keeper, and captain remind Lord Chapman that, though he has messed up, not all hope is lost.

~Probably the easiest scene to identify as being inspired by Dickens's story is where Helena hides Mary and Jim beneath the greatcoat she is wearing. These two children, cold and dressed in rags, serve to remind us that there are people struggling all around, and, at Christmas especially, we need to reach out and help.

~When Scrooge snuffs out the light of the Ghost of Christmas Past, he finds himself back in his bedchamber. He has a moment to himself, a moment of contemplation before the second Spirit appears. He is not afforded such a reprieve before the third. On the heels of the second Spirit's chastisement and immediate disappearance, Scrooge "looked about him . . . and lifting up his eyes, beheld a solemn Phantom, draped and hooded, coming, like a mist along the ground, toward him." Similarly, in this story, I have Helena, Mary, Jim, and Lord Chapman see the third and final visitor coming to see Scrooge on Christmas Eve, a man dressed all in black whose face is hidden from view.

Phrases:

There are so many wonderful lines in Charles Dickens's story, I could not help but include several in my own. Some I used verbatim, others I changed slightly to more smoothly fit into the scene. It is my hope that in doing so, readers can better see how this story follows the spirit of the original.

~"'What right have you to be merry? What reasons have you to be merry? You're poor enough.'

"'Come, then,' returned the nephew gaily. 'What right have you to be dismal? What reason have you to be morose? You're rich enough.'"

"Scrooge having no better answer ready on the spur of the moment, said, 'Bah!' again; and followed it up with 'Humbug.'"

Echo: When her Uncle Scrooge brings up, yet again, how poor Helena must be with no father to provide for her, she pushes back saying if she has no reason to be merry, he must have every reason available.

~"Keep Christmas in your own way, and let me keep it in mine." Scrooge; to his nephew, Fred, on Christmas Eve before any of his ghostly visitors appear.

Echo: The first time Helena meets with her Uncle Scrooge, she points out that he doesn't keep Christmas at all.

~"Because I fell in love." Fred; in response to Uncle Scrooge's question of why Fred got married.

Echo: Scrooge poses the same question to Lord Chapman and he responds with the simple straightforward answer, "Because I fell in love."

~"'There is. My own." The Ghost of Christmas Present, when Scrooge asks him, "Is there a peculiar flavour in what you sprinkle from your torch?"

Echo: Lord Chapman encourages Helena to help others in her own way, and not worry about how someone else may have done it.

~"Somehow he gets thoughtful, sitting by himself so much, and thinks the strangest things you ever heard. He told me, coming home, that he hoped the people saw him in the church, because he was a cripple, and it might be pleasant to them to remember upon Christmas Day, who made lame beggars walk, and blind men see." Bob Cratchit; speaking with his wife.

Echo: I have my Bob Cratchit tell Mary and Jim of Tim's unusual musings.

~"One half hour, Spirit, only one!" Scrooge; when the Ghost of Christmas Present tells him it's time to leave.

Echo: When Helena tells Mary and Jim it's time to go, Scrooge objects.

~"Spirit, are they yours?" Scrooge; to the Ghost of Christmas Present.

Echo: Helena brings two children in to Scrooge's office, beneath a greatcoat, and he asks the same.

~"This boy is Ignorance. This girl is Want. Beware them both . . . but most of all beware this boy, for on his brow I see that written which is Doom . . ." The Ghost of Christmas Present; to Scrooge when talking of the children beneath his robe.

Echo: When Helena speaks with Mary after meeting Jim for the first time, Mary acknowledges that while both her and her brother's plights are bad, his is worse than her own, for he lacks more in education.

~"Are there no prisons? . . . Are there no workhouses?" The Ghost of Christmas Present; to Scrooge by way of chastisement.

Echo: While these two options were where most orphaned children ended up, Mary admits she is desperate to avoid both.

DISCUSSION QUESTIONS

1. Most of the individuals the Ghost of Christmas Present shows Scrooge are not wealthy. They are miners, lighthouse keepers, sailors, and even the Cratchit family. Yet, they all have a very merry Christmas. In a world that keeps trying to persuade us that Christmas joy is found in material comforts, what have you found helps you stay focused on the non-material aspects of Christmas?
2. The Ghost of Christmas Present has two children hidden beneath his robe. What symbolism do you see in him having the children within his robe, instead of, say, him simply pointing out two children on the street? What might Dickens have been trying to say?
3. Continuing with the two children, the Ghost of Christmas Present labels them Ignorance and Want. Moreover, he says the worse situation is Ignorance. Of all the struggles someone might face, why do you think Dickens may have chosen Ignorance and Want to draw Scrooge's attention

to? Why does Dickens say that Ignorance is worse than Want?
4. Though the visit of the second Spirit is mostly one of joyful celebration, it becomes clear near the end of his visit that the Ghost of Christmas Present is not naive nor unaware of the suffering of many. Why, then, does he spend so much time showing Scrooge happiness and cheerful celebrations? One might argue that it would have been better for Scrooge to have a healthy dose of "reality;" to spend more time thinking of the dark, harsh lives so many face. So why might Dickens have written about a Spirit who spent much of his brief time on the earth convincing a miserly old man that there is still happiness to be found?
5. When life gets hard for you, how do you focus on the positive? How do you find joy again and reasons to stay cheerful?

He's been waiting months for her to finally notice him.
Except suddenly, he's not the only one vying for her hand.

Download the short story for free at:
www.LauraRollins.com

ACKNOWLEDGMENTS

No book is ever written without much encouragement and support from any number of people. I am forever thankful to my husband and children, as their patience and love is the reason I get to do this.

Special thanks go to my writing groups, for their advice and help. Also to Jenny Proctor and Emily Poole; without your suggestions and edits this book would not have been half so good.

Lastly, thanks to my Father in Heaven, for giving me a beautiful life and the opportunity to create.

ABOUT THE AUTHOR

Laura Rollins has always loved a heart-melting happily ever after. It didn't matter if the story took place in Regency England, in outer space, beneath the Earth's crust, or in a cobbler's shop, if there was a sweet romance, she would read it.

Life has given her many of her own adventures. Currently she lives in the Rocky Mountains with her best-friend, who is also her husband, and their four beautiful children. She still loves to read books and more books; her favorite types of music are classical, Broadway, and country; she'd rather be hiking the mountains than twiddling her thumbs on the beach; and she's been known to debate with her oldest son over whether Infinity is better categorized as a number or an idea.

You can learn more about her and her books, as well as pick up a free story, at:

www.LauraRollins.com

Made in the USA
Monee, IL
17 December 2023